KI'ASIA

QUEEN CITY'S FINEST

A Novel by

Sparkle Lewis

Published by Major Key Publishing

www.majorkeypublishing.com

This is an original work of fiction. Names, characters, places and incidents are either products of the author's imagination or are used fictitiously and any resemblance to actual persons, living or dead is entirely coincidental.

Contains explicit language & adult themes suitable for ages 16+

To submit a manuscript for our review,

email us at

submissions@majorkeypublishing.com

Acknowledgements

Thank you, God, for giving me the strength and courage to push through to my third novel. With faith the size of a mustard seed, that was all that was needed, and here I stand.

With each novel, my support changes, but these three have never changed. **Michelle Davis, Annitia Jackson, and Quiana Nicole**, I thank each of you in our own way for helping me through. I went through a lot with this novel, from losing a friend and cousin in the same week, to hitting the one-year anniversary of my grandmother's death, and then being told the doctors had given up on me. Each of you stuck through it with me and helped me overcome each hurdle. I thank all of you from the bottom of my heart. I never thought this journey would be easy, and it isn't, but with the three of you, I'll be alright! I freaking *love you ladies!*

Lawon Jones, **Jacquel Thomas, Sharena Baldwin, Ayisha Williams, and Raven Covington**, I thank you ladies for each day checking on me to make sure I was good. Whether it be a joke to brighten my day, a text or a call, y'all came through. Especially you, **Ayisha Williams**, considering you had just went through what you'd gone through. You still made time for me, and I'll never, *ever* forget you for that!

Gillian Davis, Desiree Boomer, Precious Nae, UpNorth

Chic, Michelle Ferguson, and Cynthia Boomer-Williams, hands down, y'all ride hard as heck for your girl, and I appreciate it more than you'll ever know.

To my pen sisters and those authors I ride hard with in this industry, **Vivian Blue, Chrissy J., Tiyell Barnes, Shvonne Latrice, Asia Monique', Denora Boone, my little sister Reign and daughter Virgo, the lovely Brii Taylor, Authoress Shanice, Nikki Brown,** and **Denise Barnes,** all of you have in some way inspired me or motivated me, please believe! I could have made this list a mile long because a LOT of you inspire me... but support is a two-way street.

To my cousin, **Nesha Pegues**, aka Ne'shaDaVoice, thank you so much for gracing the cover. You are a true beauty, Queen!

To my brother **George Chapman** and my sister **Deja Chapman**, I thank both of you for loving and believing in me. Thank you for never giving up on me! To my daddy, **Leon Smith**, and my mother **Patricia "Tweety Bird" Chapman**, y'all made a star—know that! I love all of you! XOXOXO!

Denytra Cunningham-Mitchell, thank you for being a wonderful supporter, proofreader, and test reader.

Touch of Class Publishing Services, LLC, thank you ladies for all you do! Continue being the best!

And last but definitely not least, my husband, **Devlin Burns (City)**, **Tanajia**, **Akeera**, **Kiasjah**, and **Khylil**, this book has been the hardest for me with everything I had to go through during writing. Y'all stood by me, wiped my tears, held me, hugged me, and let me know it was going to be OK. Even if I can't be 'superwoman' in this industry, I'll forever be y'all Superwoman. I love y'all with all of me.

To my test readers, **Sharene Price**, **Nakimba Patrick**, **Precious Nae**, **Gillian Davis**, **Brittany Page**, **Denitra Jackson**, and of course **Michelle Davis**, I thank you ladies so much for your feedback. It means the world to me. And to the readers, thank you for rocking with me. Without you, *this* cease to exist! XXXOOO!

Dedication

This book is dedicated to my children, ***Tanajia, Akeera, Kiasjah****, and* ***Khylil****. I see so much of me in each of you. All of you have inherited some part of me.* ***Tanajia****, you have a big heart but are explosive when pushed.* ***Akeera****, you have that go getter mentality, stay to yourself, and are spoiled as hell! (LOL)!* ***Kiasjah****, I hate to admit it... but you are just me; from your feistiness to your fear of trusting too much just to avoid being destroyed—you are every bit of me. My baby,* ***Khylil****, you have a loving nature and love wholeheartedly, regardless. Even at your young age, I can see the loyalty in you. I pray each day that you continue to be the prince, who will one day become the king, that your daddy and I are teaching you to be. Each of you, please keep striving for everything in life that you know you can achieve. It won't be given to you, as you already know. You know my saying: Do what you gotta do so you can do what you wanna do! I love all of you with all of me!*

A note from the author:

Although reading ***They Can't Stop Me: Return of a Savage*** and ***Unconditional Hood Love*** are not prerequisites of this book, they both mentioned Ki'Asia and the person she has become in the present (2018). This story gives you the background on Ki'Asia and what made her who she is, and also gives you more insight into Shalom aka Divine.

Before Talya and Sha... there was Ki'Asia.

Prologue

"Look, Daddy has to head back to New York now, so I want y'all to be good for your mother, you hear me?" Divine told his kids after he set his bags at the door.

"But, Daddy, we want to go with you," eight-year-old Ki'Asia whined, sitting in her father's lap. She was truly a daddy's girl, and he wouldn't have it any other way. His six-year-old son, Da'Jon, looked up at him with tears in his eyes, but he refused to let them fall. His father always taught him that men didn't cry, and he wanted to make sure that he proved to his father he was going to be the man of the house in his absence.

"I know, baby girl, but Daddy needs you to stay here and take care of your mother, OK?"

"No, Daddy, I want to go with you. Please, Daddy, pleeaasseee," Ki'Asia continued to cry. It broke his heart to hear his princess cry, but he knew he had spent too much time in Charlotte as it was, only taking two- and three-day trips back and forth to New York, and he needed to get back before things got worse than they already were. People were trying to step in and take over, and it was time for him to make an example out of them the best way he knew how.

"All right, girl, stop that crying. I will take you to visit

your daddy when school gets out," Maureen, his children's mother, said.

He stood Ki'Asia up, gave her one last hug along with Da'Jon, kissed Maureen on the forehead, and walked out the door, blocking out his princess's screams. As soon as his feet hit the pavement on the other side of the door, he was back in business mode. He looked down at his pager and saw the 911 code that was used between him and members of his crew. The cab had just pulled up, and though he was going to miss his family, getting back to New York was top priority.

***

Shalom Barron, known on the streets as Divine, felt everything he'd work so hard for was being tested. People were coming in from other states trying to take over the blocks that he had been running since the early eighties. What they didn't know was that Divine was not the one to be tested.

After leaving his girl and two kids in Charlotte, North Carolina, Divine was ready to take the streets of Brooklyn by storm. He knew what was at stake, but Divine could not let the recent actions of others go unpunished. Evidently, the out of towners assumed since he had not been in New York for the past three years, they had free rein to do whatever it was they wanted to do. There had been five fatalities in his crew over those years, and that was five too many for him. The streets would feel his pain one way or another.

For two weeks, Divine sat back and watched the movements of his enemies. He knew where they laid their heads, who resided in their homes, and the blocks they were trying to take over. Little did they know, not only was he watching, but he was mentally eliminating their existence. His thoughts became words, and it was time for those words to become actions.

On September 23, 1996, Divine and six other members of his crew posted in two buildings on Kings Highway and 98th. In groups of six, other members of his crew were posted in areas of Bed Stuy, East New York, Flatbush, and Brownsville. Simultaneously at 3 p.m., gunshots could be heard throughout each of these areas. By dusk, Brooklyn had experienced sixty-eight casualties. The borough had never undergone a mass killing of this kind. The only thing even remotely close that could compare was the Palm Sunday massacre in 1984 which claimed ten lives.

Three years in hiding and not seeing or having any contact with his kids, killed him. The murder rate in Brooklyn continued to rise, adding twenty more murders to his list. With those twenty murders also came the casualties of the eight murders of his own crew. Divine was tired of losing people and wanted it to be over.

He knew it was over for him, but at this point, he didn't care. He'd accomplished what he'd set out to do, which was eliminate anyone that threatened his empire.

The toughest battle he'd have to endure was yet to come. Tired of running, tired of hiding, Divine resurfaced in Brooklyn and let it be known. Three days later, he went to a stash location that no one knew about; not one person in his crew nor his kids' mother. He stored a few things he would need if he ever saw the light of day again. After making sure it was secured, he exited the spot and walked two blocks over to the pay phone.

"Hello?" his children's mother answered the phone.

"Maureen... baby, tell my kids I love them, and I'll see them soon. You know what to do."

I'm a B.O.S.S., G'd up yes, yes, beef I don't fret—y'all niggas is no threat.

Only thing promised in life gotta be death, so I promise on my life I'ma bang 'til the death.

I'm a B.O.S.S.

~City

Chapter 1: 2010

"Every pawn is a potential queen..."

Ki'Asia

Growing up, I always knew I wanted to be *somebody*; everybody was somebody, but I wanted to be *that chick*. I felt like it was a given right considering who my parents were. Born to Shalom Barron and Maureen Leek, you could trust and believe they were going to ensure that my brother, Da'Jon, and I continued to follow in their footsteps. It wasn't the desire for their children to become doctors, lawyers, politicians, or anything that required a degree. Nah. We were expected to become king and queen pins, regardless of whether or not we wanted it.

I had no problems with it. None at all. My brother, however, decided to go another route and attended a four-year college since he was offered a full sports scholarship for his skills in basketball. A full academic scholarship was offered to me as well, but again, that wasn't *my* dream. However, I did attend a six-month program to become a paralegal, but it was more for my benefit than that of the lawyer I was assisting. Plus, one of the professors *owed* me a job once I received my certification. It may not have been my parents' dream, but my father was definitely happy.

My pops, birth name Shalom but known to everyone as Divine, was sentenced to life in prison when I was twelve, and my brother Da'Jon was ten. He did the unthinkable and held court in the streets in broad daylight and was found guilty on two murders and being the mastermind behind twelve. They wanted to sentence him to death, but his legal team wasn't having it. People thought with him serving life, it was just as bad, but I would rather go see my father behind bars than visit his grave any day. My moms, of course, didn't see it that way.

My father's first appeal was denied eight years ago, and my mother cut him off and moved on with her life. She said that she didn't believe he would ever see the light of day again, and as much as she loved him, she refused 'to hold a nigga down that she couldn't even fuck.' Her words, not mine.

Two years after the appeal was denied, my mother

ended up getting with this dude named Walt. Don't get me wrong, Walt was a cool dude, but he wasn't my father. *Nobody* would ever take my daddy's place.

The one issue I had with their entire relationship was I knew for a fact my father expected my mother to hold him down. He basically gave her his empire to expand, but she always said she wanted to be a hustler's wife, not a hustler. She didn't mind spending the money but didn't want to work to keep the money flowing, which is how I ended up taking over all his illegal business at the age of fifteen, and his legal businesses once I turned eighteen. Considering how my mother felt, how the hell she ended up marrying Walt was beyond me. The dude owned a trucking company for crying out loud. His money was long because he owned a fleet of trucks, but still, the occupation was nowhere near bringing in the amount of money she was accustomed to.

Unbeknownst to anyone aside from my aunt Chan, myself, and Da'Jon, my father's intentions were to file another appeal with actual basis for it being granted. He never went into details of why he felt so strongly about it this time around, but I didn't care. Who would be right there waiting for him to walk out those gates would be me!

"Aight, Ma. I'll be back to check on you a little later!" I yelled to my mother on my way out of her house.

"Make sure you come back, Ki! I need to talk to you and Da'Jon about something important!" she yelled back.

I was on my way to meet up with contractors for the club I was in the process of having built. In a few months' time, I would be opening *Touch of Class Nightclub*. My father always told me to make sure I had more than one stream of income, and at the age of twenty-two, I had multiple streams, although the streets only knew of the legal ones.

On my way to the site, I called up my best friend, Desiree. She was completing her final semester at UNC Chapel Hill where she attended to obtain a Bachelor's in Management and Society with a minor in Marketing. It was perfect for me and her; as opposed to having to do an internship and trying to find a job, she was going to manage the club for me. Desiree wanted nothing to do with the drug life, but she was one hell of a promoter, which was my other clubs were so successful so far. Add that in with the fact that she was getting a degree in management, she was the perfect fit.

"What up, chick?" she answered once the call connected.

"Not shit. Getting ready to head over here and meet the contractors to go over the final details of the club. Are you excited?"

"Hell yeah! I ain't bust my ass in school for four years to come out and have to look for a job and end up having to work in fast food until something comes through. You know I'm forever grateful, sis!" she exclaimed.

Desiree and I had been best friends since sixth grade. When we first moved to Charlotte, Da'Jon and I attended private schools, but I finally convinced my mother, right around the time my father got locked up, to let us attend public school.

My first day in school, I promise I had every bit of fifteen females wanting to fight me. They said 'hey,' and I said 'hi.' So therefore, in their eyes, I was conceited all because I had yet to adapt to southern terminology. I ended up dragging a chick the first week, and when her homegirl went to jump in, Desiree quickly let her know that wasn't happening. We clicked almost immediately and had been inseparable ever since.

"But anyway, what's up wit' you? You still ain't got no dick?" she asked, and we both laughed.

"That's all ya ho ass worry about is who I'm fucking. I'm content with never fucking again for the rest of my life after dealing with these bum ass niggas down here. Fucking is overrated," I told her, and she laughed like I said the funniest thing ever.

"Sis, all it's gon' take is that one nigga to blow ya back out, and trust, you gon' be dick happy. Just watch what I tell ya. Some good dick will definitely knock yo' ass down a few notches! And maybe then, you can get over Mr. Tyleek."

And there she goes! She knew two guys were a sore subject for me, and that was Tyleek Ditmas and Tyquan Benjamin. I fell weak for the two niggas whose name started with a T; one in high school and one fresh out of high school.

Before I could respond, I saw I had another call coming

in from Da'Jon.

"Yo, sis. Let me hit you back. Little big bro on the other line, and ain't no telling how long this gon' take or what he wants."

"Aight, cool. And tell big head I said 'hey'," she replied before I switched over to his call.

"Well isn't this a pleasant surprise. What's up, bro?" I questioned once I was on the line with Da'Jon.

"Don't act like we don't talk at least once a week, sis," he said, and I chuckled.

"How's school, bro? You maintaining?" I heard him sigh and knew right then he was getting ready to tell me something I didn't want to hear.

Da'Jon was quiet all throughout school except when someone tried him, and then you saw a side to him you didn't know existed. He felt as long as he hustled, balled, and kept up his grades, everything else didn't matter. So if he wasn't in your way, stay out of his. When he left for school, I felt like I was losing my other best friend, even though he drove me crazy being protective as hell. Another reason why I wasn't out there slinging my cooch like it had no value. If a dude got two feet within my space, Da'Jon made sure the dude was pushed four feet back. And if we disagreed about it, me and him were coming to blows like we were Ike and Tina. Well, Ike and Ike, 'cause wasn't shit about me Tina.

"Man, sis... damn girl talking about she pregnant from me. I won't lie to you, I bust ole girl down a few times without a condom, but the bitch told me she was on the pill. And before you go running ya mouth, I actually *saw* her take the pill on quite a few occasions, and I made sure her ass went and got checked before I started busting her raw," he told me.

All I could do was shake my head. This would be the second pregnancy scare Da'Jon had since he'd been in school for the past two years. Him and his dick were problems I didn't need. I was about five minutes away from the site, and the last thing I wanted or needed to worry about right now was who my brother was slinging his little Peter to.

"Is that really the reason you called me, bruh? Like... what am I supposed to do? Come beat the baby out of her?

Convince her to have an abortion? What. Is. It. I'm. Supposed. To do?" I questioned, putting emphasis between each word on the end of the question.

"Nah, smart ass. If it's my baby, I know what the hell I gotta do. I called you because, you remember Tavarus that went to school with me? We called him Trapp."

"How the hell could I forget crazy ass Trapp. Yeah, I remember him. Why? What's up? He OK?" I asked, rambling off question after question. I knew how close he and Da'Jon were.

"He good. He called me and said that his homey wanted to meet with Murda. Said they only dealt with that hard body and diesel, but they wanted to add something else. I told him I knew Murda and would reach out to see what's up."

I knew Trapp hustled hard... thus the name Trapp. But dealing with that hard and heroin... people were getting football numbers. You could get away with that nose candy somewhat, but once you started including additives to brick it up, it was a total different charge.

"Who is his boy?"

“He ain’t give me a name, and I ain’t ask. He said he went to Hopewell while we were there, but by the time we were freshmen, he was a senior. Shit, maybe you know him. I don’t know,” Da’Jon replied all nonchalantly.

“So you expect me to just meet up with someone and don’t even know who the hell I’m meeting up with, Jon? Don’t nobody know who the fuck Murda is, boy! Think! Use ya damn brain. What the fuck I look like meeting up with somebody and blowing my cover?” I questioned like he’d lost the little bit of mind he had left. I loved my brother dearly, but he could act a little special at times.

“Sis... did you not hear a damn word I said? Man, Trapp will be there. All you gotta do is pick the time and place,” he said.

Trapp was like a little brother to me when he and Da’Jon used to hang out, but I hadn’t seen him in almost four years. I didn’t know who he was dealing with or anything. For all I knew, he could be working with the Feds. I hated to feel like that, because like I said, Trapp was like a little brother when he and Da’Jon hung together, but I’d come too far to allow *anyone* to bring me down.

The more I thought about it though, I was hearing Trapp's name in the streets, and it wasn't on no grimy level. He was really out there getting it.

"Yo... I just pulled up to the site. I'll think on it a little bit and give you a call back," I told Da'Jon and disconnected the call without waiting for a response. I had to weigh my options with this. Yeah, it was enough for everybody to eat, but the coke and pill territory had been mine for years, and I didn't know if I was ready to let another person eat off my plate.

Once I parked in the lot, I threw my shades on, grabbed Rosie—my pink handle 38—and got out the car. I was in awe of the progress the team had made to the outside of the club in such a short amount of time. The sign was in place, and it was absolutely stunning. When I walked inside, my mind was really blown.

I saw Carlos, the lead construction worker, and headed in his way.

"Buenos tardes, Señorita Barron. ¿Cómo está usted?"

Although my Spanish was A-1, I told his ass about speaking Spanish when we were conducting business. I was an American citizen with Black ass parents who didn't speak a lick of Spanish. I gave him a look that was more of a warning, and he smiled.

"How are you, Ms. Barron?" he tried again.

"I'm good, Carlos. Even better now that I see the progress of this place. Do I need to be moving the grand opening up?" I questioned. I honestly couldn't fathom what else needed to be done.

"No, sen... No, Ms. Barron. We still actually have a few things we need to get straight with the wiring and your office on the third floor. Also, we still have to put an en-suite in the bathroom, per your request," he informed me.

"OK, got it. I'ma go take a walk through of the other floors and see if there's anything else I want added."

As I walked through the first floor, I continued to be impressed by the development. Although I had two other clubs that were both successful, the difference with those were they were given to me and not something I'd actually worked for. With this one, it was my time, effort, planning, and detail that went in. The profits from the other clubs were solely for my father's legal expenses.

The white, gold, and black color scheme was perfect throughout. The sixteen-seater bar sat in the middle of the floor with the dance floor surrounding it. Tables aligned the left, right, and back walls of the room with the V.I.P areas directly above them. The kitchen was to the left of the far back wall, and the bathrooms were to the right. To see something I'd only envisioned come to fruition was more than a dream come true.

The second floor housed eight pool tables, two ping pong tables, two chess boards, four card tables, and seating areas. The third floor was the floor I'd be on most nights while at the club. It was designated solely for the strippers, which would have alternating nights between the males and females. I would also allow private parties for special occasions.

Now... the fourth floor was a special floor. Whereas most club owners just had special sections of the club with a curtain blocking the view for those who wanted to be 'entertained,' I had eight bedrooms built where anything could happen. As long as no drugs were involved and the girls consented to it, we were good money. Crazy, right?

I was not that club owner that washed drug money through the club. Nah. Not the main club anyway. I had the other two clubs, a butcher shop, and a funeral home. No need to bring attention to a spot I wanted to be the most profitable of all my businesses.

When I walked into my new office, I was grateful that everything was what I needed it to be—simple but elegant. The cherry wood furniture with gray hardwood floors blended just the way I thought it would. The only thing that was missing was the track lighting I requested, the electronic devices, and the dummy wall. I didn't even bother to look at the bathroom since Carlos told me it wasn't complete.

As I sat at the desk, I began to muse on what Da'Jon had called and told me. I tried to think about anybody else whose name I knew that was high on the food chain. The only person I could think of was some dude named Firm. I didn't know much about him since he dabbled in a different product, but I did hear he ran his blocks with an iron fist, much how my blocks were run. It was kind of crazy we never crossed paths, because on a few occasions,

I'd heard some of my team mention his name, but they always said he was never trying to cross over, and he respected the code as it was. So that took him out of the equation.

Pondering some more, I figured I'd let my brother Pop meet up with Trapp and his boy to see what they were talking about. Although heroin and crack weren't my thing, when it came to hustling, I was greedy. So the opportunity to expand being presented was a bonus in my book.

I picked up the glass pawn on the chessboard that was custom-made with *Murda* engraved on the side and studied it for some brief moments. Satisfied with my final decision, I called Da'Jon back.

"Tell ya boy to meet me at the funeral home Thursday at seven. After that, all bets are off."

Firm

"I told you I'll get there when I get there," I told shorty before disconnecting the call.

I really wasn't the type of dude that liked to repeat myself, but I found myself having to explain to her more times than I cared to. It was simple: the blocks don't have no hours. I didn't leave my business in the hands of others, and I had too much money to collect on these streets to say when I was coming home. After dealing with her ass for two and a half years and her knowing the type of dude I was, you would think it was embedded in her brain.

"Man, I promise you let that broad get away with too much. You can't take a shit without her ass asking is it a bitch there wiping ya ass," my homeboy Trapp said. I looked over at him, and the nigga started laughing.

"Shit, don't get salty with me because yo' ass wifed Inspector Gadget, nigga. Bitch got a GPS on the dick!" I couldn't help then but to start laughing with his ass.

He wasn't lying, though. I met Tricie one day when I had to do an out of town run. On my way out, I stopped by the gas station to get a White Owl, and this cornbread fed ass was bent over grabbing a carton of cigarettes. All I saw was ass and wasn't even thinking about the face. I knew it was too good to be true to ask that she looked presentable. Hardly ever did you see a banging body and a cute face. And if you did, you'd better run for ya life 'cause the bitch was crazy. When shorty stood up, I was hooked. She had the face and body, so that meant her ass was a nut.

However, after holding a brief little conversation with her, I found out she had a little head on her shoulders. I got her number that day, hooked up with her when I came back, and been hitting it ever since. And nah, she wasn't crazy, but her ass was definitely insecure. I'd prefer a crazy chick over an insecure one any day, especially after seeing what drove my father away from my mother.

I lived in a two-parent household up until I was nine, when my father claimed he'd walked out because, not only was my mother insecure, but her insecurities were directed because of what she was doing as opposed to what he had actually been doing. It crushed us—my sisters and I—when our father left. From there, it was like my moms started struggling. My father's attitude toward her had become cold. It was so bad, many days in the winter, we'd be without heat, and in the summer, no lights, so of course that meant no air. I always vowed that once I was old enough to do something about it, I would.

Since my age didn't allow me to move how I wanted to move, I started selling newspapers and then graduated to sweeping up in the barber shop. Little did I know, sweeping the barber shop was going to turn into the owner putting me on. But putting me on didn't just come with 'here, take this pack and make this move.' Nah, Smitty made sure he taught me everything it was to know about the game and also how to wash it through having a legal hustle. By the time I graduated high school, not only was I that nigga in the streets, but I also was training to take over my father's construction company. Now at the age of twenty-three, I was set. The only thing I needed to do was expand my territory.

Right now, I had shit on lock with North Charlotte, South Side, Boulevard Homes, and Jackson Homes, but I was only supplying diesel and rock. I wanted to add that pure white girl and pills to my list and then take over Milton Road and Tryon Hills. A ghost named Murda basically had all the areas locked with both products, and I needed to get at him ASAP. I didn't know who it was, because they ran their shit so tight you couldn't just walk over there and start asking questions. And I didn't believe in unnecessary war or bringing attention to myself, so I wasn't getting ready to start gunning down niggas in the middle of the street for no information.

As if reading my thoughts, Trapp spoke up.

"Check this, remember my homie Jon-Jon I was telling you about? Little college dude?"

"Yeah. What's good with him?" I asked, wondering where he was going with this.

"I was rapping with him, and we got to talking about this drug shit. Dude is a college boy now, but in high school, my man had the game on lock, and the nigga was untouchable. He got that damn college on lockdown as well.

Anyway, certain areas came up and he mentioned one in particular—Hidden Valley. He said he still had his connections and knew the mufucka that runs it."

This shit couldn't have come at a better time, I thought to myself.

"Aye, see if you can set that up."

"Already on it," he said with a smirk.

One thing about my man Trapp, dude stayed in the streets and kept his ears and eyes open. That's why I kept the nigga on my team. If you wanted to find out some shit, he would always come through.

As Trapp sat on the passenger side rolling up, I started thinking about my moms and siblings. Everything I'd done up until this point had been for my siblings. My father wouldn't do shit for my mother and brother, but he made sure my sisters and I always had what we needed as far as materialistic items went. I resented him until my mother sat us down and told us the *real* reason why he up and left. Not only did it put everything in perspective, but it made me look at my mother differently, and my heart broke for my brother.

Apparently, my mother cheated on my father around the time he left to go out of state for six months to build a hotel in Vegas. When he came back, he knew the child she was two months pregnant with wasn't his. He let it ride initially for the sake of keeping our family together. He treated us all the same—in my eyes—and we loved him wholeheartedly. By the time my brother was two, my father was slapped in face with the worst news ever.

While going in my mother's purse to search for his spare key, he came across some pill bottles. Never having heard of the medicine and worried about my mother's health, he took the medication to Revco to get more information. When he was told the medicine was used to treat HIV, that was the day his world ended. He confronted my mother, and she broke down and told him not only was she infected, but my baby brother was infected as well.

My baby brother died at the age of three, and my mother died four years after after when I was fourteen. My father took custody of all of us and provided us with everything we needed, but I still continued with my little jobs.

"My nigga, did you hear anything I just said?" Trapp asked, breaking me from my thoughts.

"Nah, what's up?"

"Jon just hit me back and said ole boy agreed to meet up with you Thursday at seven at Barron's Funeral Home."

"A fucking funeral home? Nigga, I ain't meeting nobody in no damn funeral home. Fuck dat shit. Nigga mind twisted. Nah, I'm good on that, man. I'll think of another way."

I snatched the blunt from Trapp and his dumb ass was sitting over there laughing. I ain't see shit funny.

"Nigga, it's just a damn funeral home. What, you scared? The dead can't hurt you. You need to be worried about these mufuckas that's walking around," he said, still laughing.

Hell, that ain't make the shit no better, but it was what it was. He stated a true fact with that. I pushed the feeling to the side and told him to hit his boy back and tell him I agreed. We had made it to our destination, so I had to block that shit out for the moment.

"You good?" I asked Trapp, making sure he had his burner on him.

"When am I not?"

As we exited the car, I spoke to a few of the dudes and chicks that were standing outside. It was starting to warm up some, so everybody was outside and in front of dude's apartment that we'd came to see. They'd clear out in a minute.

This nigga Rasheed had been ducking me for a minute now, and I was getting a little pissed the fuck off. I always kept my cool and stayed off the radar, but when it came to my dough and my fam, that cool shit went out the window. Right now, he was fucking with both.

I knocked on the door and put my middle finger up to the peephole. After hearing some movement on the other side, the chain was removed, and the door cracked open. Ole girl that came to the door looked like she wanted to shit on herself.

"Uh, hey Firm. Hey, Trapp. Sheed not here," she quickly said. I pulled the burner from my back and used it to motion for her to open the door. She looked behind her which was the wrong move, because Trapp kicked the door open, knocking her on her ass.

I turned behind me and smiled as the crowd that was

standing there previously began to disperse. Once everyone had cleared out and went back in front of their apartments, I entered the apartment and locked the door.

Now, don't get me wrong because we lived in the projects as well growing up, but just because you lived in the projects didn't mean you had to have a project mentality. Fucking apartment was stank as hell, little man was sitting on the couch with a soiled pamper, and the roaches? Oh, them niggas had to be paying rent here. It was no way in hell that many mufuckas could be roaming around and not be on the lease.

"Go sit yo' nasty, stankin' ass down," Trapp said to Monique, Rasheed's baby mom, when she got up off the floor, rubbing her ass. And it was a lot of ass, please believe, but the way those shorts rode up in it like a pair of thongs, you knew it was contaminated.

"Rasheed, Rasheed, Rasheed. Damn, man. You tried to holler at my sister and you over here got ya baby moms living like this? Damn, nigga. I mean... maybe I'd be a little more understanding of why you still ain't paid me my money if I had come in here and the shit was spotless. I would have said, 'OK. Sheed trying to keep up with the Joneses.' But nahhhh, that ain't even the case.

And you, stank ass... you don't smell that shit? Go clean yo' son up. Wait... or is that you?" I didn't know if at the moment I was more pissed about the money or the fact I trusted a nigga to be on my team that was living like this.

"Man, I ain't try to holler at ya fuckin' sister. That bitch was all up on my dick," Rasheed got bold and said. *Strike two.*

"You better not had tried to holler at her, or I'll be beating you and her ass!"

"Bitch, you won't be beating shit! You need to beat ya damn feet and clean up this nasty ass house!" Trapp yelled at Monique.

I walked over to the table Rasheed was sitting at and kneeled down to get on eye level with him.

"Rasheed... where the fuck is my money? I put you on 'cause you came to me with this sad story about how you needed to take care of ya seed and ya girl." I looked around the apartment for emphasis. "That's a lie. So where the fuck is my money?"

"Man, Firm, I'm in a fucked-up place right now, man. I got it... bu-bu-but I ain't got it all. I'm 'bout two stacks short, fam," Rasheed said, and I stood up and removed the silencer from my pocket.

"Tsk, tsk, tsk. See... the thing is, I'ma let you breathe. I'm not gon' end ya life behind two stacks. What kind of man would I be? Nah... I wouldn't do that. Aye yo, Monique, come here for a second."

She hesitated, but she walked over to where I stood as Trapp grabbed her son off the couch, holding his breath, and took him to his room.

"You love this nigga? He taking care of you?" I asked, looking dead in her eyes.

"Hell no! I mean, I love him, but he damn sho' don't take care of me, ole lying ass nigga! I been taking care of you!" she ranted, just as Trapp walked back into the little dining area with his gun in hand, laughing.

"Aight. So check this... you know where the money at that he got for me?"

She pondered for a moment, snapped her fingers, and

headed to the back. I knew Monique's type all too well. She wanted a balling ass nigga but had to settle for niggas like Rasheed because, despite her looks, she ain't had shit goin' for herself. *She lies to get taxes by saying she does hair or babysit, when in reality, she stays home and watch soaps all day, stands outside and gossips with the other little hood rats, and waits for a nigga to break her off for a piece of that stank ass shit between her legs; no ambitions or goals and feels depending on the system is her forty acres and a mule*. Bitch ain't had no loyalty to no nigga and never would. And just like money made the world go 'round, it also made bitches like this flip.

She came back to where I stood with a black cash box in her hands. I dug in my pocket with my free hand, once more, and retrieved my keys.

"Yo, where the fuck you get that shit from, Mo!" Rasheed barked on her.

"Don't you worry about it. I've been trying to break in the shit for the longest and never could," she said, rolling her neck and eyes like the typical rat.

I handed Trapp my keys, and he fumbled with the box

for a few before popping the lock.

"Firm, I promise, man, it ain't what it look like. I swear, man. Tha-that's not all mine."

I looked at dude like he was the plague.

"Forty-eight two," Trapp said, and both Monique's and my eyes popped open. *Strike three.*

Once the shock wore off, I took out what was owed to me and proceeded.

"I told you I wasn't gon' kill you today, and I'm a man of my word. Monique, you want these twenty-four stacks?" I questioned as I nodded my head to tell Trapp to head out and get my reinforcement.

Her eyes lit up like a child on Christmas Day as she responded, "Hell yeah!"

I reached in my boot and pulled out a little .380. "You know how to shoot?"

"Yup, I sure do," she said and didn't blink before ending that nigga's life. This bitch was more thorough than her nigga. Too bad she had to go.

As soon as I smiled at her, Trapp walked back in the door with my reinforcement.

Pffft, pffft!

"Tashonna, go grab the baby and head to the spot. I'll call Jackson when I get in the car."

"You got it, boss!"

Both Trapp and I walked out of the apartment, blood on our hands yet on neither of our hands... literally. I grabbed my cell phone and called up my uncle Jackson, who was a lawyer at one of the top firms in Charlotte. "Got one coming to you, Unc," I said and disconnected the call.

"Yo... you think ole boy we going to meet with Thursday gon' be the one to have those bodies?" Trapp asked as we peeled out, both of us laughing. I swear my homey was stupid.

Chapter 2

"A king may be the most important piece on the chess board; however, the queen is the most powerful as she performs more moves than any other token."

Ki'Asia

"I'm leaving out, Mr. Williams," I told my supervisor after I shut down for the day. I was glad I only worked in the law office on Tuesdays and Thursdays, because more days than that would drive me up the wall. The only reason I was here was to learn as much as possible about the law for my own personal reasons.

"OK, Ms. Barron. Next week will be a light week. I'll probably only need you to come in one day, but the week after, I'll need your help to prep the files for that upcoming case you started on last month," Mr. Williams said, coming from his office.

"I got it. See you next week." I grabbed my purse and hurried to the door. Mr. Williams' ass gave me the creeps. He was a nice looking older man, but he was too intimate for my taste... always wanting to give someone a hug or gently touching their back. I shuddered just thinking about it.

I had to hurry up and get home to change. The meeting with Trapp and his 'boy' was this evening. Once I found out exactly who his 'boy' was, I was beyond eager to meet with him. To hell with letting Pop handle this one. But I wouldn't lie, I was extremely nervous.

As soon as I pulled up in the driveway, I hurried and jumped out the car and ran into the house. I had less than an hour and a half to get dressed and head across town to the funeral home. On my way up the stairs, I made a mental note to call my mother since I never made it back over there the other day. What she had to talk to me about couldn't have been too important because she hadn't tried to contact me since.

I ran to my room, went in the closet, and grabbed the first thing I saw, which was a pair of Gucci jeans, the belt, a peach short-sleeved Gucci shirt, and the jacket. After throwing it on the bed and damn near ripping off the dress I had on, I went into the bathroom, pinned up my hair, and turned the shower on. While the water was adjusting, I removed a washcloth and towel from the linen closet, all the while talking to myself, trying to prep for this evening.

As soon as I stepped foot in the shower, my body immediately relaxed. I allowed the water to wash away the built-up anxiety and fears of the unknown. Could I really go through with this? Did I want to step into a territory I knew nothing about? During visits to my father and Aunt Chan, we always spoke about the ins and outs of the coke industry, and eventually, my auntie schooled me on pills, but never did we discuss heroin on any level, and my father always told me the difference between bricking up and keeping shit in powder form. But then I remembered the reason I even agreed to this meeting. Not only was it an expansion for this person, it was an expansion for me as well. And trust, their expansion would be minimal compared to the takeover I was strategizing.

Mind on business and reservations pushed to the side, I stepped out the shower in grind mode. I knew what I wanted and what I had to do to get it. After getting dressed and texting my godbrother, Pop, to tell him I was on my way, I stepped in my heels, grabbed my purse, and was out the door.

When I got in the car, I looked at the time and instantly got pissed. That must have been one hell of a shower, because I had less than fifteen minutes to make a half-hour drive. I pushed in Jay Z's *The Blueprint 3* CD and rocked out.

***

Knock, knock!

"Sis, they here," my brother said as he peeped his head into my office.

At ten minutes to eight, these niggas finally wanted to show up. They had better been glad I had some business to take care of here, because they definitely would have been assed out.

I stood up from behind my desk, as I did if I were greeting a family coming to make funeral arrangements, and waited for them to appear.

When I looked up, the butterflies in my stomach immediately started fluttering, and I felt like the high school girl that had the biggest crush on the man in standing in front of me. Trapp noticed me before his friend had a chance to look up, and when he did, his mouth dropped.

"Oh shit," Trapp said in shock.

It was then that Tyleek looked up from his phone and stared into my eyes. *Whoa, Kemosabe. Little Storm down there thumping!* Fine was an understatement for this dude. I mean, life had definitely been good to him.

Tyleek was by far the finest nigga at Hopewell High School. He was around six one, had waves for days, the most beautiful smile I'd seen on a dude, and his daily attire, though simple, put every dude to shame and made them want to be in his shoes. He and I dated in high school for about a year, but I couldn't handle, not only the whores that flocked around him on a daily, but the shit he had between his legs. The nigga took my virginity, and I should have never wanted sex after that.

I hadn't seen Tyleek in almost two years, but the last time I saw him, I remained unseen to his eye. I scoped him out at The Capital Grille while I was celebrating my mother's birthday with her, Da'Jon, Walt, and Desiree.

He didn't see me—I made sure of it—but I'd definitely seen him. I also wanted to make sure I stayed out of sight because of the chick he had on his arms. Ki'Asia Synese Barron didn't do unnecessary drama, and with the difference four years had done my body—stacked it in all the right places—I was sure it would draw his attention as it did 80 percent of the men *and* females in the restaurant. The butterflies I had in high school every time he'd walk in my direction, returned.

"Yo..." Tyleek started, but it was as if he couldn't verbalize his thoughts. Trapp, on the other hand, ran over to my desk and picked me up, spinning me around.

"Boy, would you put me down, yo' silly ass!" I laughed because Trapp used to do that when we were younger. Every time he saw me, he would pick my short ass up and spin me around.

"Ki... what the fuck you doing here? You ole boy's receptionist?"

I looked at him, confused as hell.

"Um... who is ole boy, and whose receptionist am I supposed to be?" I mean, I was genuinely confused. Then it hit me. *Murda.*

"We supposed to be meeting up with someone here about some... umm... some shit," Trapp said, and I burst out laughing. Tyleek was still stuck, squinting his eyes like he was trying to figure out could it really be me.

"How the fuck I didn't catch on to that shit! Barron's Funeral Home. Well I'll be damn!" Trapp said like he'd really figured out a mystery of some sort.

"I guess I'm ole boy then, because Jon hit me up and said you told him someone wanted to meet with Murda, but he didn't tell me who the person was because he said he didn't know. But anyway, how have you been, Tyleek?" I questioned, diverting my attention toward him.

His eyes narrowed before a smile graced his face.

"Ms. Ki'Asia muthafuckin' Barron."

And he remembers.

"Man, you know her?" Trapp asked the question I was thinking.

"Let's just say Ki'Asia and I have a little bit of history. She used to be my little boo in high school until she up and stopped fucking with a nigga. Ain't that right, Ms. Barron?"

He and I both laughed, and I thought back to the one sexual encounter we had. Quickly, I had to force myself to think about something else. I couldn't handle what he was offering back then, but I knew I could do a little something with it now.

"True indeed," I replied.

He continued looking at me with that smile, and I had to turn away to keep from showing that I was blushing.

"Alright. So you two came to talk business. Have a seat and let's get to it," I said, waving my hand frontward, gesturing for them to sit.

It was taking everything in me to look up at him. And my feelings were indescribable because every emotion I thought I had put to rest about this man was back in full throttle. Even the way I used to admire his swag with the simplest of an outfit. If it had been on any other dude wearing what he had on this evening, I wouldn't have given it any thought. But the gray Nike sweat suit with them butter Timbs was doing something to me. It had been two years since Storm had been tamed, and trust, she was ready to act a whole fool on some dick, even though I kept trying to deny it.

"First, I want to apologize for us being late, and thank you at the same time for waiting for me. Got caught up in some bullshit I needed to handle real quick. So thank you, gorgeous," Tyleek said then licked his lips and sat back in the seat.

"You good. So what can I do for you?" I questioned, back in business mode.

"Well... shit, my bad, ma. I just can't believe this shit," he said, running his hand over his face before laughing briefly.

"So check it. Right now, I—"

"Supply heroin and rock to all of the areas that I don't supply. However, there are two areas that you and I bump heads with. You're known in the streets as Firm. You deal with a cat named Felipo from Colombia, and he only deals with heroin and nothing else. You get ya hard from a little local cat up in Baltimore. Ditmas Construction is, although profitable, a front for you and your way to wash and move your product on a heavier scale. You, without the construction business, are worth 4.2 million, and that doesn't include the stocks and bonds that you have in your name and your sisters, Taysia and Anise.

You also have a fund set up, which is another way you wash, in the name of your little brother, Dedrick Ditmas—which, by the way, I am sorry for both losses. Your father, Tyrone Ditmas, retired earlier than he had to and gave the construction business to you. And you were brought into the game by Mr. Godfather himself, Smitty. I could go on, but do I need to?"

I sat back and crossed both arms over my chest. *Checkmate*.

Just as I knew they would, both of them sat there with dumb expressions on their faces.

Since Da'Jon didn't have any information for me, I decided to do a little investigating myself and found out that Trapp ran with the dude Firm, whom I knew for a fact was heavy in the game. From there, I did a complete background check and found out that Firm was actually Tyleek Ditmas, my first and only 'boyfriend' here in

Charlotte.

After a few brief moments of silence, Tyleek decided to speak up.

"Well damn. You know all of that, do you know who all on my payroll?" he inquired with a laugh.

Honestly, I did, but I wouldn't let him know that. He was beating around the bush with the business aspect, and I was ready to get into it.

"The reason I wanted to meet up with you is exactly what you just stated. I want to expand and start tapping into that white girl and pills. Considering you and I push separate product, I could have easily set up shop in your areas, but that's not how I roll. I don't believe in bringing attention to myself or starting unnecessary beef when I can just go to the source and come up with a compromise that will be beneficial to us both.

The way I see it, we eating off the same plate anyway. But, I do wanna dip my hands into some other things." He leaned back in his chair, and I thought about what he said. I knew I wasn't willing to let him deal with coke in no areas that I ran, but at the same time, I wouldn't mind adding more product in the mix without having to get my hands dirty, and more territories.

Tapping on the desk with my nail, I was still in deep thought about it. The only person pushing coke on my territory was going to be me, but... we could both expand.

"Let me ask you a question. How do you feel about expanding outside of Charlotte? Say maybe Greensboro, Winston, Salisbury—take ya pick."

"Nah. Right now, I feel comfortable with where I'm at," he answered too quickly.

I chuckled a bit before responding. "Then I guess you have your answer, Mr. Firm. It was good seeing you again, though. Trapp, stay in touch with me, sweetie. Just because Da'Jon's gone doesn't mean you have to stop coming around." By this time, my arrogance was showing. The way I looked at it, I had something he wanted. He could either agree to my terms, or he could try to strongarm my territories, which wouldn't be too smart on his behalf.

See, what people outside of my circle didn't know was that although Murda ran this empire—who was still incognito—I still had the backing of my father. I had males and females set up through different areas of Charlotte and surrounding areas. Hell, I had people looking over me that I didn't even know existed but would pop up when needed most. The people I dealt with directly were Biggz, my godbrother Pop, my cousin Preme, Raquan, Nutty, and Mone. Biggz himself had several teams up under him, and then everyone else had their team. And it wasn't limited to Charlotte. Nah. This was an east coast thing.

"You still got that little smart-ass mouth. I guess my mans ain't tame you enough. But chill out. I ain't say all that. However, I need to think on it a little bit. I don't too much care for stepping into unknown territory, and that's exactly what you're proposing. I like the way you handle business, and I wouldn't mind fuckin' with you... on many levels, but umm... that ain't a decision I'ma just roll with," Tyleek said.

Trapp looked at me and started smiling, noticing that, once again, I was blushing. As bad as I didn't want to turn his initial offer down, knowing I would have the chance to be around him, I had to make moves based on business and not my hormones or feelings. I was never one to make permanent decisions based off of temporary emotions, and just because Storm wanted some dick right now, that didn't mean she was going to control my life!

"I can accept that. Well, gentlemen, if we are done here and there's nothing else to discuss..." I grabbed a sticky note and pen and wrote my number down. "You can call me when you've come to a decision. It was good seeing you both," I said, reaching my hand out to shake Firm's.

Of course, crazy ass Trapp ran around the desk, picking me up and spinning me around before Firm could accept the handshake. Once he put me down, what came from Firm's mouth took my breath away.

"Now come give daddy a hug. Fuck that handshake."

My mouth dropped, but I quickly gathered my composure. I slowly walked around the desk and into his opened arms. *Storm... don't start your shit. Is that his... Oh my goodness! Is that his dick?* He was swaying me back and forth with no room between us. You couldn't even slide in a sheet of paper. When I felt his dick brick up in his pants, I had to pull back.

"OK. So I'll be waiting for that call. Again, good seeing both of you." He looked at me and smirked before licking his lips and winking, then he and Trapp headed out the door.

I walked back around my desk and sat down, butterflies still running rampant in my stomach. I leaned my head back and closed my eyes, and before I could get in a zone, I was interrupted by a knock on the door. Thinking maybe Tyleek and Trapp had come back, my eyes quickly popped open to see Pop.

"You good, sis?" he asked before sitting down in the chair Firm had just occupied minutes ago.

"Yeah, bruh. What's up? What you got for me?"

"It seems like you and Firm both have a common enemy. This nigga, Dreek, wants to take over everything. I had my boy doing a little investigating, and the nigga is more of a mystery than you are. Nobody knows anything about him aside from the name Dreek. I mean, we don't know where he lives, his family, no nothing. You need to holla at your boy the next time you speak to him. Maybe he knows who this nigga is. Did y'all come to an agreement on some terms?"

Pop was throwing too much at me at once. I didn't like dealing with 'ghosts.' I was one of the most carefree, easygoing people ever, but I liked to deal with all situations head on. Just like Tyleek came and set up a meeting, if any nigga in the street had an issue, my doors were always open. Now... one may not have had the opportunity to deal with me directly, but again, my doors were always open. My guns always bust as well, so whoever this Dreek person was, I hoped he knew what he was up against.

"Nah. I gave him my personal number and told him to get back at me. He wanted to do exactly what I thought—add coke to his inventory and expand in my territories, but I ain't with that sharing shit, bruh, feel me?"

"Most definitely. You think he gon' be a problem?"

I thought on it only for a quick second. "Doubt it. He's not the confrontational type, and like he said, he could have just attempted a takeover without coming to me first. He got a little solid team of niggas up under him—shit, females too. It's crazy 'cause it's like the nigga's a male version of me," I stated with a laugh.

"That can be good or bad for business," Pop said as she stood up to exit the office. "But come on so I can walk you out. Don't want you texting me talking 'bout you hearing noises in this bitch," he said, and I fell out laughing.

He knew me all too well, because every time I was here alone, I swore up and down something was after me.

This Dreek cat was weighing heavily on my mind. I didn't need the bullshit right now with me trying to get this club opened up and possibly expanding. Just more bullshit on top of bullshit.

Firm

When I walked into the office of the funeral home, word is bond, I expected to see some dude sitting behind the desk. I was too busy in my phone arguing with Tricie's stupid ass and wasn't paying attention. When Trapp said, "Oh shit," and I looked up and saw who it was, it almost put me on my ass.

Back then, shorty didn't know it, but she could have had my heart. I knew she along with everyone else assumed I was this male whore, but that was the furthest thing from the truth. Yeah, I had chicks flocking around me left and right, but I couldn't control that. Only two of them could even say they'd sampled the dick. Now when I got out of high school... well, I was single. Different story. Still, I had never run into another female that had me open like Ki... except for one—Denice.

Ki'Asia was by far the baddest chick in, not just Hopewell, but damn near all of Charlotte. Shorty stood at about five three and had a body that made you wanna stay on your knees in prayer to avoid temptation, even while in high school. Now? Lord have mercy. Let's just say God was playing a cruel ass joke on me. I didn't think it was possible to get any finer than she already was, but that dark skin with them slanted hazel eyes, full, pouty lips, big perky ass titties, and ass that wouldn't stop, had only gotten better over time.

I remember before I graduated, I said I was going to wife her, but my homeboy told me she was fuckin' with some cornball dude, so I didn't pursue her again. I wasn't in the habit of breaking up happy homes. Come to find out, she wasn't dealing with anyone, and his ass was the one that wanted to push up on her. I beat that nigga's ass for three days straight when I found out. By then, I'd already graduated and was on to other things. She never left my mind though. I just didn't have a way to contact her, and since she hung by herself, except for with the one chick Desiree, I couldn't even reach her through a friend. The last number I had for her was changed. Never in a million years would I have expected her to be a face I ran into this evening, and especially not the face behind Murda.

"Earth to your spaced-out ass! What you over thinkin' 'bout?" Trapp asked. I almost forgot he was in the car.

"Yo, how much you know about Ki'Asia?" I inquired.

He looked at me and burst out laughing.

"My nigga, focus on Tricie. You ain't ready for that. Ki'Asia liable to whip yo' ass! She legit on that bullshit, for real. It don't even surprise me where she at wit' it right now. She always had that feisty mentality when I used to chill with Jon, and those two used to fight head up like two bulls locking up. And the girl pushed them thangs better than any nigga I knew.

I don't know why it didn't click with me when Jon said the shit, that it was Ki'Asia he was referring to. I guess I thought she would have been doing something else more... ladylike. I mean, you *do* hear her name all over the radio, right, my nigga? Ki'Asia Barron, the club owner, the funeral owner. I mean, shit, shorty got her hands in everything. And she's a fucking queen pin. Ain't this some shit!"

When he said that, though he was still laughing, it was true. I knew in school she was smart as hell, so I wondered what made her decide to run an empire. Before I could speak my thoughts, my phone rang, interrupting me.

I looked down and hit the damn steering wheel. I swear this chick was starting to piss me off.

"Yeah, Tricie?"

"Boo, what time are you coming home? I miss you!" she said, and when we first met, that shit would have made me drop everything I was doing. Now it made me want to push her in front of an eighteen-wheeler.

"If I have to tell yo' ass one more time... The streets don't have no fucking hours! Damn! You know when I leave the office, I'm in the streets. Why do you keep insisting on calling me asking the same dumb ass questions like my answer gon' change for you?"

I heard her sniffling through the phone, but I didn't feel bad for her. Tricie had the game fucked up if she thought I was going to let her tears affect me in any way. I'd never even told shorty she was my girl. She was just a chick I let lay up at my spot since I knew I was getting another house built.

She was an easy fuck, obedient, looked good on the arm, sucked the hell outta some dick, and even though I laced her, she wasn't in my pockets like that. I gave—she never asked.

"You don't have to talk to me like that, Tyleek. I just asked a question," she said, still sniffling.

"Look, I think I'm just gon' chill with Trapp tonight, aight? I'll hit you up tomorrow to take you to lunch," I told her, disconnecting the call. I turned my phone off after that because I didn't want her hitting me back up, crying and being all dramatic.

Trapp looked at me and laughed harder than he was laughing prior.

"Man, what the fuck is so funny?"

After catching his breath from damn near passing out from laughing so hard, he said, "Nigga, yo' ass just want Ki. Any other time, Tricie wouldn't have bothered you like that. You already know what it is with her, so you're immune to the shit. But now that you done saw Ki's fine ass, you in ya feelings!" he yelled out, laughing again.

I ain't even try to dispute it, because he was 100

percent correct. A chick like Ki'Asia, I wouldn't mind having in my corner. She was already on, so she knew the game. I doubt I'd have to assure her every hour on the hour that I was coming home. The shit got tiring.

When we pulled up to Trapp's crib and I parked, I could have sworn I heard someone arguing.

"Yo, man, you hear that?" I looked at Trapp and asked.

Instead of replying, he reached in his waistband, pulled out the hammer, and cocked it. Without asking any questions, I did the same. No soon as Trapp stepped up on the porch, four shots were let off, and both Trapp and I took off running up the steps. Neither of us were prepared for what was behind that door.

Sprawled out on the living room floor was Trapp's sister. I ran through the house to the back door and saw a figure with a black hoodie and jeans jump into a gold colored Camry on the next street over. Running back to the front of the house, I took off, headed toward the corner to try and catch the car, and ended up shooting out the back windshield. Somehow, I caught the license plate number.

I pulled my phone from my pocket and scrolled through the contacts. "Yo, Cam. I need you to run this plate number for me ASAP," I called and told my connect at DMV. "And I'ma hit you back later with a name I need you to get some information on for me," I added then disconnected the call.

I didn't even wanna go back to the house and face Trapp. The connection he had with his sister was the same I had with mine, so I knew his soul was crushed right now.

Trapp lost his parents in a car explosion when he was in middle school, so his sister, Sabria, became his caretaker. She was only twenty-five at the time, had just been diagnosed with Lupus, and put her life on hold to take care of her younger brother. Trapp had cousins, aunts, and uncles, but he wasn't close to them at all, and no one could take the place of his sister. She was all he had left.

When I walked back in the house, Trapp was standing against the wall, looking down at his sister's body as tears flowed from his eyes. In the few years I'd known Trapp, I'd never seen him express any emotion. Seeing my homey like this fucked with me hard. I glanced down at Sabria's body and shook my head. We were talking about a girl who didn't fuck with nobody, so whoever did this shit needed to be dealt with ASAP.

I wasn't going to ask Trapp no dumb shit like 'you all right?' knowing damn well he wasn't. So I just stayed quiet and let my homey release his emotions through tears.

***

I'd been trying to keep Trapp's head on straight for the past three days. He'd been smoking and drinking heavily, and I was worried about my boy, especially since Cam informed me that the car came back as registered to someone in Texas and had been reported as stolen. After we made the funeral arrangements yesterday, Trapp basically shut down.

It was Sunday evening, and I was finally headed home. Trapp said he couldn't take being in the home he and Sabria shared, so he asked if he could stay down in the basement, and of course, I didn't have a problem with it.

When I pulled up to my house, there was a car parked in the driveway that looked vaguely familiar, but I couldn't place it right off the top of my head. Tricie ain't really fuck with too many people, and her parents didn't like me, so I knew they weren't coming to visit. Shit, I couldn't stand their uptight asses either, and they didn't know how much I wished she would take her ass back home to them and just drop by and break a nigga off every now and then. Their bourgeois asses were the reason she was so clingy, if you asked me.

Once Trapp and I finished facing the blunt we were smoking, we jumped out the car, and I set the alarm. Even though I stayed in a middle-class neighborhood and parked in the garage, I still kept my shit under lock. Jack boys always found a way to take what they wanted.

We entered the house through the garage, and it was dark as hell. Now I was really stumped as to whose car was in my driveway, because it didn't even look like Tricie was home. I couldn't blame her. I guess she got tired of waiting for me to bring my ass home. I turned the light on in the living room and told Trapp to make himself at home, threw him the remote, and headed up the steps. The closer I got to my bedroom, I heard what I thought was talking. *I know damn well this girl didn't leave the TV on,* I thought to myself.

When I got to the room, I paused because I heard a voice ask whose pussy it was. *I'm bugging the fuck out. I don't know what the hell Trapp had in that damn weed, but I don't want no more of that shit.* I chuckled and opened the door to my room, flicked the light on, and for the third time in three days, got the shock of my damn life.

"Bitch, what the fuck!" There, in the middle of my bed, was Tricie's home girl, Janice, getting fucked from behind with a strap-on by none other than Tricie. Yo... I promise if I wasn't so pissed, I would have pushed Tricie's ass out the way and showed Janice how it felt to be fucked by some real wood instead of some plastic, ole lesbian ass.

"Nigga, who we got—" Trapp ran in the room, gun

drawn, and paused midsentence at the sight before him. He looked over at me, face turning red, and I could tell he was getting ready to go in. All of a sudden, the nigga fell out laughing.

"This ain't the time, nigga," I told him, pissed as hell. I mean, his dumb ass was laughing so hard, he was holding his stomach and had tears coming from his eyes. I didn't know if I was still high or what, but I couldn't do shit but laugh with him. Shaking my head, I focused back on the scene in front of me, but it felt good to see my homie laugh for the first time in a few days.

"Oh my goodness, Firm, don't kill me," Janice's snow bunny ass said. Yeah, shorty was as pale as Casper. "I'm leaving," she added, keeping the sheet wrapped around her like nobody had seen what she was trying to hide.

"Nah, y'all go ahead and continue. Hate I interrupted. When y'all finish, Tricie, you can get ya shit and leave with her, ole carpet munchin' ass." I was pissed the fuck off right now. I mean... nigga wanted in on the action.

Trapp followed me down the steps, laughing the

entire time.

"Nigga, what the fuck? Yooooo, why you ain't tell me Tricie get down like that?"

I looked at him with my head cocked to the side. Dude was straight up clowning at my expense.

"So just fuck the fact I said this ain't the time, right? You just gon' sit there and keep clowning, right? And you supposed to be..." My speech trailed off as I felt my phone vibrate in my pocket. Pulling it out, I looked at the screen and saw a number I didn't recognize.

"Who dis?" I answered.

"Damn, that's how you answer the phone?" Ki'Asia's voice said on the other end.

I had to look at the phone for a brief moment because she gave me her number, but I never gave her mine. Then I thought about it; she knew everything else, so her having my number shouldn't shock me at all.

"My bad. A lot of shit been going on, shorty, and I didn't have a chance to store ya number. I ain't forget about you though. What's up?"

"I need to meet with you to discuss a potential 'issue'

that concerns us both. Is there any way you can meet with me tomorrow... say around the same time?"

What potential issue could she and I both have? I was curious, so of course I wasn't going to turn down the meeting. Before I could respond, Tricie's ass came down the steps, crying and screaming like she'd lost her mind.

"Firm, can we please talk for a minute? Please, Firm, I can explain!"

I looked at her because I knew this shit was coming. She was getting ready to start with that crying and the overboard dramatics, and I ain't have time for it. I just wanted her to get her licky licky ass the hell on somewhere.

I put the phone down to my side against my pants so Ki'Asia couldn't hear what I was getting ready to say.

"If you don't get yo' nasty, trifling, pussy eating, hitting a bitch from the back with a strap ass out my damn face, I'ma go against my morals and knock the shit out yo' ass!" I barked. It only riled her up more.

"Baby, please. We can talk about this. I promise this was my first time. I... I wanted it to be a surprise for you.

I know every man wants a threesome. Firm, don't make me leave, please," she said, then started bawling. I knew it.

I knew I joked about it previously and said what I would do to Janice, but one thing about me that my sisters could bet their bottom dollar on—I don't stick my dick in white females. Not racist or anything. But a pink on pink twat does nothing for me.

"Tricie, have some damn dignity and get to stepping out the door. You knew what it was gon' be when I saw that. Step."

"You don't have to talk to her like that, Firm!" Janice got in my face and yelled. I knew this bitch had to have lost her damn mind.

Before I knew it, her hair was wrapped around my hand as I dragged her ass to the door.

"Bitch, get the fuck out. Disrespecting me by bringing yo' ass in my house and getting... wait, would it really be fucking if the dick was plastic, rubber, whatever the hell it was?" I turned around and looked at Trapp and asked. My nigga was laughing so hard, he was damn near hyperventilating. I turned my attention back to Janice, threw her on her ass, and pushed her little carpet munchin' best friend out the door behind her, then slammed it. I could hear Tricie knocking, crying on the other side of the door, but I couldn't care less.

Again, Trapp's ass was on the couch laughing his ass off, and all I could do was shake my head. Just that quick, I forgot Ki'Asia was on the phone. I put the phone back up to my ear just to hear her laughing as well.

"Ha... ha... ha... shit's hilarious to y'all, huh?"

"I'm sorry. I must have called you at a bad time," she said as she continued laughing. Her laugh and voice were making my dick hard as hell, and I needed to get her ass off the phone.

"Yeah, aight. You good, ma. But yeah, I can do that. Where you wanna meet at?"

"I'll let you choose this time. Text me the location," she said, still laughing, and disconnected the call.

I guess today came with good and bad. I found out Ms. Perfect wasn't perfect after all, and I didn't have to do a thing to get rid of her. Trust me, it was on my mind, because after seeing Ki'Asia the other night, one way or another, I was determined to make Ms. Barron mine.

Chapter 3

"When you see a good move, look for a better one."

Ki'Asia

"Good evening. I'm an attending party for a reservation of two for Ditmas," I told the hostess once I walked inside of Capital Grille. It was funny that Tyleek had chosen this spot to have a meeting.

"Right this way," the bony blonde said as I followed behind her.

When we reached the table, Tyleek was already seated, but stood immediately once he saw me, and pulled the chair from the table for me to have a seat. *Mm... a gentleman... I like*.

As soon as the hostess walked off, the waitress came to the table to take our drink orders. Once she left, I looked over Tyleek's appearance which was much different than the last time I saw him. This time, he was rocking all black everything, except for the Ferragamo belt he had on, which had the red symbol. I refused to sit here and talk Storm out of something tonight. If he wanted it, he could for damn sure get it.

Tyleek must have caught me looking him over because when I looked up to make eye contact, he had the most arrogant smirk on his face.

"Like what you see, ma?"

Unlike the other time I saw him, that blushing, shy girl role went out the window. This time I looked him square in the eye and said, "I do."

He must've been taken back by my response. Leaning back in the chair, he simply crossed his arms over his chest and smiled.

"Where's Trapp tonight? I know I didn't ask for him to come with you, but I figured he'd be here since we were discussing business."

Tyleek dropped his head, and my antennas went up.

"Is everything OK? What's going on with Trapp?" I asked, concern lacing my tone.

He rubbed his hand over his face and shook his head. "He's in a better headspace, so that's good. But umm, his sister was killed a few days ago, and we walked in right after the nigga shot her. I don't know how much you know about Trapp, but his sister was his everything, ya know? My dude fucked up right now, so I didn't wanna throw no business shit his way," he told me, and my heart immediately broke for Trapp.

I remembered meeting Sabria when Trapp and Da'Jon first started hanging out, but I didn't know her too well. Da'Jon did tell me that he and his sister were real close and that his parents died in a car explosion, but that was the extent of what I knew about her. However, what I was getting ready to tell him wasn't good at all, and I hated to be the bearer of bad news.

"Oh no. I'm sorry to hear that. I was aware that they were close, so I can only imagine what he's going through. Make sure you tell him that I'm here for him if he needs anything, and he has my condolences."

"I got you, ma. Aight, so let's talk business. What's good? What you needed to speak to me about?" Tyleek leaned up, placing his elbows on the table.

"I was informed that you and I had a mutual rival. A man that goes by the name of Dreek. I've done my research on him and can't seem to find out anything about him, which is a first. I was hoping maybe you could lead me in the right direction," I informed him.

He became more serious than I'd ever seen him.

"What makes you think I got issues with a nigga named Dreek?" he questioned.

"Tyleek... by now, you should know if I want to find something out, that's what I do, even though finding out shit on this nigga is damn near impossible. Like I said, the information was brought to me. Umm... I found out more recently that he was getting ready to target your crew."

He stared at me long and hard, tongue rolling around in his mouth on occasion. Right before he got ready to respond, the waitress came back to our table with our drinks and took our order. Tyleek ordered the Bone-In Ribeye while I opted for Seared Citrus Glazed Salmon. We also placed an order to share mashed potatoes and creamed spinach. Once the waitress walked off with our orders, I got back down to business.

"Yeah, I know the fuck nigga, and you do too. We went to school with him. He was a year ahead of me though, so he was two years ahead of you. I'm familiar with the nigga's territories, which is why I said I didn't want Salisbury or any surrounding areas. And trust me, I attempted the shit before, the areas the nigga got on lockdown, and his team didn't budge for shit. Trying to get any information on him or even setting up a meeting is impossible. And the crazy part about it is he ain't on my level and damn sure ain't on ya level. He does his little thing with weed and pills and is on a small scale with coke. But his territories are widespread, and his team locks his shit like Fort Knox. Like they protecting the damn president or some shit.

Different from how I approached you, right when I became heavy in the game, like I said, I wanted his spots. I wanted to expand quickly. Me and my team, and it was ten of us, rolled through one of his blocks up in Salisbury, and started a war. I ended up losing three good ass men," he said, and I could see talking about it bothered him.

"That's the reason I told you at the first meeting that I'm not the confrontational type. Before I start a war, I'd rather ask for what I want. If I feel that's getting me nowhere, well, then it is what it is. But on the other hand, if you're hearing that this nigga is a mutual problem and he's getting ready to target me and mine, then you know something I don't know."

I knew not everyone moved like I moved, but I needed to make sure Tyleek was as official as I needed anyone on my team to be. When you were in this line of work, you needed to make sure you had your eyes and ears to the streets at all times. If he wasn't even aware of who his enemies were, I had an issue with that.

"So after you attempted to take over one of his territories, did you think it would stop there? I mean, how could you not consider him an enemy after you shot up his blocks?" I questioned.

"Honestly, there's no logical explanation for that. I lost three total. But he lost three for every *one* I lost. For a year, I was on alert, and the nigga ain't made a move, so I assumed he was one less person I had to worry about. But don't sleep on it. Every move I make is carefully thought out, so when Dreek's blocks were hit, that didn't point back to me. Unless he's just finding out now, there is no way he could have known who it was.

I don't leave signatures, and nothing I do is repetitive. Even my stash spots are switched up twice a week. My niggas move around monthly, and I stay adding and subtracting. And when I have to subtract, trust me, I subtract to where it's removed completely," he informed me.

I knew Tyleek wasn't green to the game by far, but I truly needed someone who handled business the same way I did. When the waitress brought the food to the table, Tyleek and I decided to put business to the side for a second to enjoy our food with more mild conversation.

"So, Ms. Ki'Asia, tell me what's been up with you since school. I see you have your empire and the funeral home, and your name is ringing bells in the street with ya clubs and all. What else you got going on?" he asked.

I was glad that he was taking an interest into finding out more about me on a personal level, because once we started discussing business again, I would know whether or not he could prove himself.

"Well, in addition to the funeral home, I also have a

butcher shop, two clubs, *Club Essence* and *Mirage*, and I'm in the process of opening up my biggest club, *Touch of Class Nightclub*. The other two clubs are straight for the partygoers, but Touch of Class will be on another level. It's going to have something for everyone. And... believe it or not, I am a paralegal."

He almost choked on his food when I said the last part.

"Wait, so you mean to tell me that you literally got your hands in both sides? Don't get me wrong, I got cops, lawyers, and a few politicians on my payroll, and I do some other illegal shit, but never in a million years had I considered something legal on the law side. Smart thinking though, ma. That's a good look," he said, causing me to blush at his compliment.

"Thank you. So what else have you been doing with yourself since you graduated, aside from the construction company? Maybe I missed some information when I did my research. And yes, I'm nosy, so I'm asking as well, who's the lucky lady in your life?" I was feeling all kinds of bold this evening.

"I knew that was coming up," he said, and he and I both

laughed. "Aside from that, nothing. The construction business actually takes up more of my time than many people would think. I'm there every day handling new clients, hiring for crews in locations when we go out of state, and all the day-to-day operation. Between that and hustling, I don't have time for much else.

And as far as a lucky lady, I guess you heard that conversation the other night, so you already know. Had a little shorty I was kicking it with for about two years, but I just never felt the connection with her to completely give her me... Tyleek. She got Firm, feel me? I smashed, dropped some dollars on her and all that, but I could never give her my heart. Hell, couldn't even make her my girl. And since we're on the subject, what up wit' you? You not gon' sit here and tell me somebody as fine, intelligent, and has everything going for herself such as yourself, is single."

Knowing when I told him this he wouldn't believe me, I had to find a way to convince him without him thinking I was lying.

"To be truthful with you, I've never been in an actual

relationship aside from the one with you. That ain't to say I'm some saint. I've just never found a man to match me intellectually. I'm a sapiosexual, so what's appealing to the next woman does not appeal to me. I don't like arrogant dudes that feel their looks, dick, and money are supposed to make my world go around, which was you, minus the money back in the day. I want a dude that respects and understands my lifestyle; one that knows how to lead but allows his woman to play her role as his support as well and the leader if need be.

I don't want a man that's so caught up in feeling the man has to be the head that he forgets, without a strong woman on his side, he is nothing. Those are the types of men that I've run across, and I've never been the type of female to play the background. I'm front and center or by my man's side, but I'll never play the background for anyone," I told him before taking a sip of my water.

His eyebrow raised, and I could tell I'd put something on his mind, which was exactly what I wanted to do. My father always told me that if a man couldn't accept the woman I was and what I brought to the table, he was not the man for me. I had a list of niggas that wanted to *be* with Ki'Asia but couldn't *handle* what came with being with a woman of my caliber. The crazy part about it was that men that had as much going for themselves as I had, never tried to approach me. It was always low-level hustlers, wannabe gangsters, or men old enough to be my grandfather, which didn't attract me at all.

Once we were both finished with our meals, we ordered another drink, and I got back down to business.

"Back to the business at hand. I'm glad I decided to meet up with you because I was hitting a dead end with this situation. I've been dealing with it now for close to six months.

Evidently, this dude is thinking expansion as well because he's trying to send me a message. Some months back, he hit Tryon Hills, and last month, he came through and shot up Brook Hill. It's crazy, because he never does it when I'm out there, which leads me to believe it's not like my cover is blown on who Murda is. I'm thinking he has some sort of death wish or either he doesn't know what he's up against. No one has ever tried to strong arm my territories. When those became my areas, I let it be known, and it wasn't anything nice. I know no one knows the face behind Murda, but people know enough not to touch Murda's areas," I told him.

On the low, I was getting pissed off, but Firm didn't need to see that side of me yet. He was getting ready to say something, but my phone vibrated on the table, and I saw it was my mother calling.

"One second, Tyleek. Let me take this. It's my mother," I told him before getting up and heading to the restroom. I didn't know why I felt the need to explain who it was, but I did.

"Yes, Mommy," I said when I answered the call.

"Don't damn 'yes, Mommy,' me, Ki'Asia Synese Barron. Didn't I tell yo' little bubblehead ass I needed to talk to you and your brother? I swear, y'all think 'cause y'all grown, I won't knock the hell out of y'all!"

I snickered, and she went the hell off! She didn't realize her rant was making me laugh even more. I stood at the mirror in the bathroom, looking over myself, as my mother went on and on. When she said the word 'marriage,' I tuned back in to the conversation.

"You said what, Ma? Who's getting married?"

"So you really gon' sit there and basically admit you ain't heard shit I said. I told you that me and Walt got married. That's what I wanted to talk to you about. I wanted you to be a witness for us. We went to the justice of peace, and now I want to hold the reception at one of the clubs," she said.

Now I see why she'd been blowing me up. It wasn't a big deal that she'd married Walt or whatever since they'd been together for so long, and my father had started seeing someone else as well from what I'd heard, that had been holding him down recently.

"Of course, Mommy. I'll set everything up for you. How about in the next two weekends?" I asked. Time was winding down for the opening of TOC, and I really didn't have much time to do it any other time.

"That's perfect, baby, and thank you so much. Where are you at right now? I'm ready to start planning. I'm excited, girl!"

"I'm having a business meeting right now, so I'll have

to hit you back a little later. And I promise I'll call you, Mommy," I told her before ending the call.

When I got back to the table, Tyleek was keying away on his cell. I sat down and immediately jumped back into the business side of conversation.

"So, Tyleek, I'm figuring that since you know his territories, you already have some playing field advantage. I need you to find out anything else you can get for me. I have a feeling that the shit that jumped off between you and him is not over, and I know for a fact that what he's pulling with me is not going to fly.

I need the heads up on him before he makes another move, feel me? I know you said it's hard to get any info on this dude, but I need something ASAP, and by any means necessary."

"I got you, ma. So business aside... when you gon' let me take you on a real date? This was cool and all, but I want to get to know my future wife all over again," he said, and I had to smile.

"You just focus on the business at hand, and let's see how happy you make me. Then we can go from there.

Bet?"

He looked me in the eyes before shaking his head up and down, smiling.

"Don't act like you ain't fazed by a nigga, ma. You remember. You know how ya little friend reacts when I'm in your presence," he whispered as he leaned in closer to the table. "She still go by Storm?"

My mouth formed an 'O' before I dropped my head. If this nigga only knew what he was doing to me.

Firm

"For dust thou art, and unto dust shalt thou return."

Sabria was loved by many. So many people had come out to show their respects and say their final goodbyes. I even saw Ki'Asia and her little brother, who I remembered once I saw him. I went over and had a few words with her immediately after the funeral, on some business shit.

My dude Trapp was hurting bad. As everyone walked away from the burial site, he continued to stand there silently as the tears rolled down his face. I couldn't say anything to comfort him because I didn't deal with death well at all, but I did let him know that I was here for him.

After half an hour passed, he finally decided to leave.

"Yo, I saw you talking with Ki after the funeral. She agreed to the terms?"

The last thing I wanted to discuss with him right now was business. He wasn't even aware of what was discussed at the meeting the other night. He had enough shit to deal with, and the last thing I wanted to flood his mind with was the fact this nigga Dreek could be coming after us.

“I already see the look on ya face, bruh, and I know what you’re thinking. I’m good. It’s killing me inside, but I know Bri wouldn’t want me to stay stuck in a bad headspace, mourning her death. Life goes on, and I know she’s always here with me. Not in the physical, but she’ll forever live through me.

So talk to me. What’s good?” he asked, and I sighed before going into detail.

“The meeting I had with Ki’Asia Monday night... she wanted to discuss a mutual rival. Thing is, *we* had no idea it was even an issue. And I still don’t know if it is for us because Ki’Asia didn’t go into details outside of the fact that she heard the nigga was getting ready to target our team.

She wants me to be the one to get info on this dude. So I’m gonna meet up with the crew a little later and also talk to my uncle Jackson and crooked ass Black at the police department. I don’t want you in on this at all though, bruh. You got too much shit to deal with,” I told him.

Noticing he had zoned out a little bit, I was getting ready to question him until he asked me some shit I hadn’t even thought about.

"Yo... if he's targeting us, you think it's possible he could have had something to do with Bri's death? It ain't farfetched," he said, and he was right. Generally, one of the rules of the streets was no kids and no women. But these days, niggas didn't care. They'd touch your grandmother if it meant causing you pain.

"Hmm... it's possible, fam, but the fact that she was arguing wit' ole boy when we pulled up makes me think it was more on a personal level, feel me?"

"I forgot about that shit. You right. Aight, but check this. I'm not sitting back not doing shit. If I'm not putting in some kind of work, my ass will go crazy sitting up in the damn house. Besides, you never know what's going to pop off. Don't act like you don't need me, nigga," he said, and I laughed.

We jumped in the car and headed to the repast at Ebenezer Baptist, where the funeral was held. At first, Trapp was saying he didn't want to go be around a bunch of fake muthafuckas that didn't even deal with Bri when she was alive. But I got him to see that after today, he didn't have to deal with them at all. He was a grown ass man on these streets, and the only person that looked out for him, aside from our crew, was Sabria. She's gone now, so if he told them all to kiss his ass, that was his God-given right.

"Aye, man, I really appreciate you looking out. You didn't have to allow a nigga to stay with you and shit. I don't know what I'ma do about the house, but I can't stay there, man. Too many memories," Trapp said.

"No worries, fam. You good. We'll look into putting the house up for sale and getting you into something else ASAP. But for now, you know you can stay with me as long as you need to. Don't go getting all mushy on me either, nigga," I told him, trying to lighten up the mood. Little did he know, once my house was finished being built, I was going to give him my spot as a gift.

When we pulled up to the church, it was as packed as the funeral was. Black people always attended something with free food, regardless of the reason.

Once we parked and got out the car, I saw Ki'Asia and her brother walking up the steps. I didn't wanna be loud as hell and call shorty, and I didn't have to; Trapp's retarded ass made a scene.

He ran up behind her and scooped her up, spinning her around as soon as she got on the top step of the church.

"Boy, didn't... I... tell... you... to stop... that... mess!" she yelled, hitting him between words. All of us started laughing except for her.

"Almost gave me a da—heart attack. Lord, he almost made me curse! I promise you ain't got the sense the good Lord gave you!" She shook her head and laughed with us.

"But for real, how are you holding up? You need anything?"

"I'm hanging in there. And I'm good, ma. I don't need nothing. What's up wit' you, boy?" Trapp asked Da'Jon.

"Chilling, fam." He nodded his head in my direction. "What up, man? You Firm, right?" he inquired, and I nodded as we dapped each other up.

"Yeah... I'ma be your future brother-in-law," I said, causing Da'Jon and Trapp to burst out laughing, and Ki'Asia to drop her head, blushing.

"Man, let's go ahead in here and get this shit over with.

Oops. Forgive me, Lord," Trapp said. My boy was straight up retarded.

When we got to the dining hall, everyone started hugging Trapp and asking him the normal questions that they knew were inappropriate but chose to ask anyway. Somebody even had the audacity to ask what he was going to do with the house. People had no fucking filter and regards to a person's feelings.

I kept stealing glances at Ki'Asia 'cause shorty was looking right. She had on a baby pink dress with the matching blazer and some silver studded heels that made me wonder how the hell she could even walk in them. Now wasn't the time to be thinking inappropriate thoughts, but the way that dress hugged her little five-three frame made me wanna give that pearl between her legs a tongue lashing.

I hated to be thinking sexually every time I got around her, but shit, it was what it was. Every time I saw her, I reminisced on how her walls grabbed my dick back in the day. She was the first girl whose pussy I ate, and the last. But seeing as how she pulled a Linda Blair on my ass, I had to be doing something right. I must have zoned out because she snapped her fingers in my face twice.

"My bad. What's good, ma?"

"I asked did you have anything for me yet," she said barely above a whisper.

"I'll have you by next week, and that's my word," I told her, and we got back to eating.

Trapp was holding up pretty well, despite the circumstances, but I could tell that he, just like I, would be glad when this day was over.

A week later

"Aight, this what we got, y'all. I need y'all to be on alert and ready for whatever. Some of y'all are not aware of the shit that popped off the beginning of last year with the nigga Dreek, but I'm hearing he's gunning for us. Keep the routine switching up, and make sure y'all stay strapped at all times.

Yayo, what's the word on that shipment?" I asked my

top runner. Once I met with the connect, Yayo was the one that ensured everything was straight.

"That new boy came in and I set up a few test runs. Man, niggas is straight fienin' for that shit."

"Good, good, that's what I like to hear." In addition to straight diesel, I was sampling that tar to see how it worked out, so I was low-key happy as hell shit was working in my favor.

"Since everything good, I'll get at y'all niggas later. I got some other people coming through. Oh... and y'all need to recruit more soldiers. Ain't no telling what we up against, and we need to be prepared at all times."

After everyone nodded or spoke their confirmation, they grabbed their hard hats and headed back out the door. I had a team of forty-six dudes, and we were expanding daily, but I only dealt with my top six on a regular. The less the street runners knew, the less business would get out.

"I just saw Black pull up," I told Trapp, who was sitting there facing a blunt like he didn't hear what I said.

"Nigga, did you not hear me say that Black just pulled

up? Put that shit out!"

"Man, fuck Black! Ain't nobody thinking about his crooked ass. Hell, he might ask for a pull. Watch this shit."

As soon as Black walked in, he scrunched his nose up in the air like he was smelling something foul.

"I see somebody puffing that good shit. Let me get a hit," he said, and I just looked at Trapp and shook my head. I didn't know how he knew, but he knew.

"So what you got for me, Black?" I asked after he and Trapp finished smoking.

"Well first, Dreek's real name is Andarius Cuthbertson. Why the hell he goes by the name Dreek, I don't know. Next..." He slid a folder in my direction, and I opened it up. What I saw threw me for a loop to say the least.

"Andarius R. Cuthbertson, born to Mildred and Frank Cuthbertson of... Dallas, Texas. Moved here his freshman year of high school. Sister, Darlene Brigman, still resides in Texas."

As I went through the file, I saw all types of assets

that were in his sister's name, pictures of thc family, addresses, everything. But the one that stuck out to me the most was she owned a 2008 Toyota Camry. I immediately thought back to the Camry that I saw the night Bri was killed.

"There's more," Black said, handing me another folder. The contents of the folder baffled the shit outta me.

"Yo, Trapp. Who Bri was fuckin' with?" I asked, and he looked at me with a dumb look.

"She wasn't fuckin' with nobody, nigga. The fuck you ask me that for?"

I didn't want to, but I slid the folder over to him. I knew he had read it because his ass turned a different shade of black.

"Where you get this shit from? This ain't true!" he yelled as he slapped the folder on the table.

"But it is. Dreek has a brother named Branden that Sabria has been dealing with for almost six months. I don't know her reason for not telling you, but I'm assuming it's because of Branden's past. Branden came home from prison two years ago after serving five years in prison for sexual intercourse with a minor. Now I'm not sure if Sabria knew this or not, but anyone who has access to the internet can pull it up. He's a registered sex offender," Black relayed to us.

"So shouldn't he be considered a suspect? If you knew all this shit, why the fuck ain't nobody locked up yet!" Trapp barked.

Black and I both looked at him, understanding his frustration but wondering had he lost the little bit of mind he had left.

"Trapp, think, man. I know this shit fucking with you. But you want them to handle it or us to handle it? Pick a poison."

He didn't say anything else; just sat there, shaking his leg.

"Aight. So you got an address for me, I'm assuming," I said, redirecting my attention back toward Black.

Like I knew, he came through. Once he gave me the information I needed, he exited the office, and I looked over at Trapp.

"We gon' get this nigga, bruh. That's my word."

I hit Ki'Asia up and told her I needed to meet up with her ASAP. She texted me back and I told her to meet me at her club over off Factory.

"Aye yo, Trapp, let's be out," I told him as I snatched my keys out the desk drawer along with the folders that Black gave me. Trapp walked out ahead of me, and I locked up and set the alarm.

The ride over to Ki'Asia's spot was quiet, each of us in our own thoughts. I needed to know how to connect the dots. The only thing that made sense was Dreek found out it was me that hit his spots and decided to come after not only us, but anyone affiliated. How his brother played into it is what I needed to figure out.

After pulling up to Ki'Asia's club, I parked and went to jump out the car.

"Wait, man. Let me holler at you for a minute." Trapp grabbed me by the arm. "Look... I know you're supposed to be giving information to Ki and all, but I wanna do that nigga myself. I feel like I deserve that shit, man. He took my heartbeat from me. He can't die by nobody else's hands, feel me?"

"Nigga, you ain't even had to stress that to me. That nigga's yours."

We jumped out the car and walked up to the doors of the club. I went to open it and it was locked, but I peeped a little buzzer on the side. Once I pressed it, I heard the door click to grant us entrance.

I'd never been here, but the shit was nice as hell. She had a little chocolate and crème colored theme going with a nice size dance floor. It wasn't the biggest, but it was straight. I noticed she had two bar areas; one looked to serve alcohol, and the other had a menu. *That's different*, I thought to myself as I walked over to the bar with the drinks. I could use a shot right about now.

"Hey, fellas. What can I get for you?" the bartender popped up from behind the bar and asked, damn near scaring the shit out of me. My mama used to tell me that meant I wasn't living right. I ain't even expecting nobody to be behind the bar since the club was closed.

"Let me get a Henny and Coke, Houdini," Trapp told her before I could even place an order, causing me to chuckle.

“Dude, you stupid, I swear. Let me get a double shot of vodka, ma.”

As the waitress walked off to fix our drinks, Ki’Asia seemed like she appeared out of thin air and stood before us.

“Yo, y’all do magic tricks in this club or some shit? Or y’all just like scaring the hell outta people?” Trapp asked with a serious look on his face.

“Shut up, boy! What’s up, Tyleek?”

As I always did when she was in my presence, I looked her over, surprised that she looked straight up hood, nothing at all like she did the last few times I’d seen her. Them jeans looked like they were painted on her body though, and she had on a damn fitted hat with her hair hanging down. Beauty at its finest.

“You the only person that can get away with calling me my government, ma,” I said, as I reached out my arms for a hug which, surprisingly, her short ass walked right into.

She sat down at the bar between me and Trapp.

"Keesh, let me get a Goose and juice!" she yelled out to the bartender. "So I'm assuming you got something for me since ya text said you needed to meet with me ASAP."

"Indeed, I do," I told her, sliding her the folders.

She sat there, slowly reviewing the information from both folders, sipping her drink, while Trapp and I had already demolished three.

"Where did you get this from?" she questioned.

"I got a crooked from the PD on my payroll," I told her, and she nodded her head.

"Well, it's only one thing left to do." She spun around, facing me.

"Some of this information I knew, but some of it came as a shock. I know you're the man in what you do, but I also needed to see how you would handle the back end of things. In this game, we have to be aware of our surroundings, as I'm sure you know, but we also have to be five steps ahead of our enemies. If not, we're always vulnerable for an attack.

With that that being said..." She stuck her hand out to

me. “Welcome to the team, partner. I agree to your terms *only* if you agree to partner with me.”

Shit, she ain’t said nothing but a word. I reached my hand out to shake hers but ended up pulling her into my arms and tonguing her little fine ass down. The fuck she thought?

When I released her, she looked up at me and smirked before looking over at Trapp, then her eyes grew wide.

“Trapp, don’t do it!” she yelled, but he picked her up from and spun her around anyway. I had a feeling this was going to be the start of some major shit... for business and personal.

Chapter 5

"How well you play the game of life comes down to the sum of your choices. Whatever you decide, don't be the chess piece, be the chess player."

Ki'Asia

Tyleek must not have known I would grab his ass, take him to the office, and fuck the hell out of him with the way I was feeling right now. Storm was begging for a release, and he wanted to keep teasing me.

After we celebrated with a few more shots, went over the details of this partnership, and I told him who the key players were and how we moved, we decided to head out. I was a little tipsy, Trapp was damn near falling over, but Tyleek was standing strong. Once Keesh left, the guys and I locked up and were making our way to our cars. It was a little after midnight, and the night breeze felt good on my skin; however, something didn't feel right for some reason, so I looked around to make sure everything was good, then patted my waistband for my burners.

As soon as I turned around to speak to Tyleek, I heard tires screeching and saw Trapp pull his gun out, on point. Tyleek damn near threw me behind him once he saw the passengers of the vehicle with windows down and guns out. A multitude of shots were let off before the car came to a slow stop at the end of the street. *Glad I wore sneakers today*, I thought to myself as I treaded toward the car, both guns drawn, with Tyleek and Trapp following behind me. My brother Pop and his team were already there.

Once I made it to the car, there were only two passengers alive, struggling to breathe. I immediately recognized one as Branden, Dreek's brother. We needed him alive in the worst way, plus, Trapp needed to do the honor of ending his life. I aimed at the backseat passenger and put one through his head. I went around the car to the driver's side and did the same for both of the men sitting in the front and back, although they were already dead.

"Take 'em to the butcher shop and then to the funeral home. Pop, get rid of the car. Trapp, grab this bitch ass nigga and put him in the trunk. I hope his ass will make it," I instructed the team before lightly jogging back to my car.

I pulled up beside them so Trapp and Tyleek could load the fuck boy into the trunk. “Tyleek, y’all meet me at the funeral home,” I said before peeling out.

I needed a blunt bad as hell. These niggas had to be watching Firm because no one knew Murda and Ki’Asia were one in the same. And the only person I knew could be gunning for him right now was Dreek, and that didn’t sit with me too well, especially when you came shooting up my shit, putting me in danger. Where he fucked up at was he didn’t know Tyleek was with Murda, and Murda had eyes on her at all times.

My phone vibrated, but I wasn’t in the mood to deal with anyone right now. I’d see who it was once I reached my destination.

Half hour later, I was pulling up to the funeral home. Once I parked, I grabbed my phone to check and see who called. Seeing it was my mother, I quickly dialed her back.

“Yeah, Ma, what’s up?”

“I was just checking on you and making sure everything was straight with the reception,” my mother said, and I could hear the aggravation in her tone.

"Mommy, I do this for a living. Trust me when I tell you, I got this, OK? Your reception will go down as one of the greatest in history," I informed her.

"OK. Well, where you at now? I know it's late, but you can come over here, and we can discuss colors and—"

"No, Ma. *I* got this. And I'll hit you up tomorrow. I'm handling some business right now. Love ya!" I rushed her off the phone and disconnected when I saw Tyleek pull up behind me.

I waved him to pull up beside me under the carport, which had a side entrance into the funeral home and also an entrance to the basement. When him and Trapp got out the car, I popped the trunk and headed to unlock the cellar door leading to the basement. Once I pulled it up, Trapp and Tyleek grabbed Branden's body and followed behind me.

I flipped the lights on once I got to the bottom of the steps and pulled a chair to the middle of the floor. This wasn't gon' take long anyway, unless Trapp had some torture ideas in mind.

As soon as they set him in the seat, Trapp hauled off

and punched the shit out of him. He was barely responsive, but that didn't stop Trapp from wailing on his ass.

"Trapp, man, hold up. Let's try to give him a chance to explain what he knows. If you keep whipping his ass like this, you'll never find out the information you need to," Tyleek told Trapp.

My heart broke at the sight before me because I couldn't imagine something happening to Da'Jon and I found the person responsible. It would be no telling what I'd be liable to do.

Trapp's chest heaved up and down, but he stopped swinging. As I got a good look at the dude, I realized his ass could have made it. He'd only been shot in the shoulder and leg. No telling which gun did the damage and if the bullet traveled, but he'd be alive long enough to tell Trapp what he wanted to know.

Once I saw that the dude was nodding off, I went to the closet and grabbed a bag of ammonia sticks. I popped one and put it under his nose, which caused his head to jerk up. I was ready to get this shit over with.

Trapp grabbed another chair from the corner and sat in

front of Branden.

He sat there for a good little minute with his head down before he spoke up. When he looked up, tears were puddled in his eyes.

"I just wanna know why, man? What the fuck my sister do to you for you to kill her?" I could tell it was taking everything in him not to break down.

"Aggghhhh... Man, fuck you and ya bitch ass sister. And you, Mr. Firm—my brother gon' kill... aggghhhh... He gon' kill yo' ass!" he said before spitting out blood near Trapp's foot. I prayed that Trapp would let it slide so he could make this nigga talk.

I stood off to the side and let them handle it. Trapp smiled the most devious smile I'd ever seen on someone. He snapped his fingers and left the basement then came back in moments later with a book bag.

"Yo, ma, you got a little table down here or something?"

I went back into the closet and grabbed a folding table, wishing all the while I had a bag of popcorn. This was getting ready to get real interesting.

Trapp spread a cloth on the table and laid out all types of crazy stuff. He had a scalpel, boning knife, rubbing alcohol, and some stick pins. *What the hell is he getting ready to do with stick pins?* I wondered.

After Trapp put on some thick latex gloves, he sat back down in the chair in front of Branden and picked up the stick pins. Tyleek smiled and reached in the bag and grabbed some handcuffs and rope. Once he secured the dude's arms behind the chair with the cuffs and tied his feet to the chair, Trapp started back his line of questioning.

"Let's try this again." He put the stick pins in a circle around each of his knee caps, then grabbed the scalpel and cut off the area within the stick pins. Before grabbing the alcohol, he peeled the skin that had been cut and then proceeded to pour the alcohol over it.

Branden started screaming and cursing, and both Trapp and Firm were standing there calmly. I actually found the scene rather comical. This was some shit I would do.

"Again... Why did you kill my sister, Mr. Branden? I got all night, and I don't mind seeing a muthafucka suffering, so trust me, you will give out before I do."

"Arrggghhhh... man... arrrrggghhh." Branden grunted through his pain, and once he collected himself, began speaking. "Man, my brother wanted me to holler at either Sabria or Anise. I chose Sabria because that Anise bitch was too stuck up. Hell, at first, he wanted me to get at Ki'Asia, but I wasn't about to holler at Divine's daughter," he said, causing my head to jerk up immediately.

"How the fuck you know my father's name!" I yelled. Trapp had better hurry up and end this dude's life before I took the pleasure from him.

"His name was mentioned before in our meetings, and I did my research on him. I don't know what connection they have to your father, but he was mentioned. And best believe, Dreek also knows you're Murda. Anyway, Sabria was the easiest one to get close to. I played on the fact she had Lupus since my mother passed from it, and I knew all about it. That's all I'm telling you," he said and put his head down.

"Bullshit! You gon' tell me whatever the fuck I ask," Trapp said as he repeated the same procedure on his left leg as he did with the right. I, on the other hand, sat there completely shocked. It wasn't possible for people to know I was Murda. It just wasn't possible.

By the time Trapp finished, we found out that Dreek wanted to, not only expand to Charlotte, but take over the entire drug industry in Charlotte. In addition, I was never supposed to be a casualty. Yes, Dreek wanted to take over my territories, but he wanted to do it by eliminating everyone under me. I found that hard to believe since they came to the club shooting, not knowing who was going to get hit. He also told us that only Dreek knew who Murda was and for some reason hadn't shared it with anyone on his team except for him. Poor Sabria was just a pawn in the nigga's sick ass game.

"And the fucked-up part about all this is, the way you did my sister is the same way your fuck brother did you. He ain't give a fuck about you. If he did, he would have made sure you didn't come for one of ours," Trapp said before he pulled out his gun and emptied the clip in Branden's body.

"Damn... I ain't even get to use the boning knife. That's my favorite part," Trapp said like he was really hurt.

I didn't know how others did things, but I didn't leave room for error. I pulled good old Rosie out, walked up to Branden's body, and let off three shots to the head. As I went to walk off, Tyleek grabbed me by the arm and pulled me back.

"You feel that shit? You been bossin' the fuck up all night, and he the one having a reaction, ma," he whispered in my ear, referring to his brick-hard dick poking me in my backside. Here he was thinking about sex like there wasn't a dead body in the room. I was trying my hardest to keep it on a business level with Tyleek, but Storm was purring her ass off, and I also knew that I'd been wanting this man for the longest.

The relationship we had back in the day was cut short on my behalf, and there was no telling where we'd be now. Being young, prideful, definitely not insecure but not having time for bullshit, I allowed other females and their attraction for him to run me away. I always vowed to myself that if I ever had the chance again, there was no way in hell I would let anyone, or anything interfere. I was determined to make this man mine, again.

I did something that shocked both me and him. I reached behind me and gently grabbed his dick through his pants before slowly turning around.

With my free hand, I reached around his neck and pulled his head toward me then whispered, "All you gotta do is say the word. I'm waiting." I kissed his full lips then walked off, leaving him there with his mouth opened and Trapp laughing.

Shortly after, he and Trapp followed me outside, and I locked the door to the cellar after shooting Pop a message telling him there was a spill in the basement that needed to be handled.

"So since we partners and all, let me finally get that date I asked you about," Tyleek said, opening my car door.

"That's a bet." Once I was seated, I waved bye to Trapp, and Tyleek kissed me once again before hopping in his car and pulling off.

***

After my mother made all that noise about me doing a reception for her, the chick had the audacity to cancel on me at the last moment. I was good and damn pissed. How you call somebody and cancel three days before the event? Now I had all this extra inventory of party supplies and customized items I couldn't do anything with. I boxed the customized items up and took them straight to her house.

"Ma, you here!" I yelled out after letting myself in. The weather had done a 180, but you couldn't tell that by walking in my mother's house. Sweat beads were popping all over my forehead. I set the box down and rounded the corner to the kitchen where I saw my mother at the stove. I kissed her cheek and took a seat at the table.

"It smells good, Ma. What all you cooking?" I asked, just to make conversation.

Honestly, my mother and I didn't have your average mother/daughter relationship. We co-existed on earth and tolerated each other. I loved her dearly, but when she turned her back on my father and did God knows what with his money, I saw her in a different light. She also blamed me for things that were beyond my control. It was almost like she hated me at times, but the feelings became mutual when she said fuck Shalom Barron. No one says fuck Shalom Barron.

When she gave me money over the years, it was always for one purpose and one purpose only: product. With the profits made, she assumed I was taking the money and buying clothes and jewelry and other materialistic shit that didn't mean anything to me and giving the rest to her. But nah... I was walking in my father's footsteps, per his blessing, of course. Any clothes or jewelry I wanted, I'd hit my aunt up in NY and have it sent to me at Desiree's house. When she caught on to what I was doing, she tried to put a stop to it, but by then, I was my own woman, doing my own thing. Plus, it was her who always told me these were the 'dreams and goals' she had for me. There was no use in trying to stop it once I took over where my father had left off when we moved down here.

It wasn't just my money—don't get me wrong. Once my pops got word to my aunt Chan and Biggz that he approved of what I was doing, everything else was a piece of cake.

"Chicken, cabbage, rice, green beans, and cornbread. You want a plate?" she asked, and I was never one to turn down food.

"Sure," I responded before heading to the bathroom to wash my hands.

When I got back to the kitchen, my phone chimed, alerting me of a text message. I looked down at my phone and saw it was Tyleek.

That Nigga: *I'm ready for my date, shorty. I wanna spend the day with you Friday. You game?*

Me: *Friday is good. What time and where?*

That Nigga: *I'll come scoop you up, if you willing. Be ready by 8 that morning.*

Damn! When he said spend the day, I didn't take it literally.

Me: *You weren't lying when you said all day, huh? Pick me up from the club. I'll be there.*

It wasn't that I didn't trust him to know where I stayed, but I had a few locations. When I got off work from the law firm Thursday evening, I knew I needed to head to the club, so I was staying at my spot close by.

That Nigga: *See you then. And oh, I got two more new boys that's ready to go out. Send Pop or Preme.*

Me: *That's straight.*

I shot Preme a text relaying what Firm said, which was basically two shipments of heroin had come in that needed to be distributed. I placed my phone back in my purse and looked up to my mother whose face was scrunched up.

"What?" I asked.

"Who got you smiling like that? Gotta be some dick 'cause I know you ain't smiling like that over no cat," she said, and I burst out laughing. I hadn't even realized I was smiling until she made mention of it.

"Nah, it was just a new business partner, that's all. He gave me some good news," I replied.

"Oh, OK. Something with the club?"

"Something with the streets."

"I don't see why you won't just focus on the clubs, the funeral home, and the butcher shop. Shoot, even the paralegal position. You got all that going for you, but you still wanna run the streets like a dude," she stated, and I had to bite my tongue to keep from going off on her. I loved her, but she wasn't getting ready to tell me how to live my life when she was the one that basically forced me into this life.

"Maybe one day, Ma. Where's Walt?" I asked, changing the subject.

"I know what you're doing, but it's all good. He's on the road. That's the real reason why I had to cancel the reception. We'll just do something here in the backyard when he has some time... if he has some time," she said, and I sensed a hint of sadness in her voice.

Not ignoring her, but hungry as hell, I got up to fix my plate and grabbed a bottled water out of the refrigerator before returning to my seat.

"Ma, talk to me. Is everything OK with you and Walt?" I asked, drowning my chicken in hot sauce.

"Yeah, baby. Definitely. It just gets a little lonely at times when he has to go on the road. But we're good. He's actually thinking about coming off the road and letting his guys handle it while he does local routes."

That's what her mouth said, but I wasn't convinced.

Yet, I wasn't going to push the issue. If something was going on and it was meant for me to know, she'd tell me in her own time.

She got up and fixed her plate and came back to the table, and we sat talked for about an hour. I helped her with the dishes and straightened the kitchen back up, and then we retired to the living room.

I reached over and grabbed the box of items that I had purchased for her and Walt. All of the items were customized with *"Walt and Maureen Lemon. April 6, 2010."*

"Ma, I decided to give you these since I couldn't use them. These are the items I had ordered," I told her, reaching in the box and pulling the items out one by one.

The items ranged from crystal glasses and plates, to photo albums and jewelry boxes. She actually had tears coming from her eyes, which was something I hadn't seen since she had to tell Da'Jon and I that our father wasn't coming back.

"Aww, don't cry, Ma. Look at you getting all emotional."

I did something I hadn't done in forever and reached over and gave her a hug.

"I can't believe you had really done all this for me. I know we don't always see eye to eye, but... You know what? Forget all that. Let's just enjoy this day. You wanna watch a movie with ya momma?" she asked, which shocked me, and as much as I would have loved to have a bonding moment with her, the shit just felt awkward. My mother *never* wanted to spend time with me unless she really had something to talk to me about.

I was a female that always trusted her instinct, and my mother's vibe was throwing me off right now.

"I tell you what, Mommy. I'll stay with you and watch a movie if you agree to tell me what's really going on with you. Deal?"

In less than 2.5 seconds, her whole attitude switched up.

"Look, just like you don't want me in your business, stay outta mine. Now deal that! Oh... and thank you for the gifts. You can see your way out," she said before she got up off the couch and headed toward her bedroom.

One would think I'd be more shocked by that, but I'd been dealing with Maureen's bipolar ass for twenty-two years. That definitely didn't shock me. *That* was the Maureen I was used to. As concerned as I was, I remembered about her wellbeing, this was just the type of relationship we had, and I had to deal with it. I did just what she said—saw my way out. To hell with her.

Chapter 6

"A king always has his queen's back..."

Firm

I made sure I was up bright and early. I had the whole day mapped out for me and Ki'Asia, which even included plans on taking her to meet my sisters. Even though we weren't a couple, I knew she was it for me, so taking her to meet my sisters and getting their approval was a must. I'd take her to meet my father another time.

After handling my hygiene, showering, and throwing on my clothes, I texted Ki'Asia to let her know I was on the way. Our first destination was going to throw her off a little bit, but if I knew her like I thought I did, it would definitely set the tone for the day.

I pulled up to the club at 7:52 and texted Ki'Asia again to let her know I was outside. Three minutes later, she walked out the club, and as always, she was dressed to impress... in heels. *Why didn't I tell her to make sure she didn't wear heels?* I thought to myself.

As she made her way to the car, I got out and gave her a hug and sneaked a kiss on the cheek before opening the door for her.

"Where are we off to?" she asked as soon as I got back in.

"You'll see. I should have told you to skip the heels, but umm..." I looked her over and bit my bottom lip. "I ain't complaining."

On the way to our first destination, we talked about any and everything under the sun. I knew it was going to be a long ride, so I was prepared for it. Plus, I wanted to get to know the grown Ki'Asia as opposed to the little fly high school girl.

Talking to her, I found out we had more in common than I thought. She loved football and boxing but disliked anything basketball and baseball, which was me. I knew she was from New York originally, but I never knew why she moved down here. When she told me about her father, it all made sense as to why she questioned Branden the way she did. Her father was somewhat a legend in NY, and if you were in the game and didn't know the name, you needed to step ya game up.

As we talked, never once did she ask where we were going. But when we pulled up in front of a warehouse in the middle of nowhere, she looked at me like she wanted to choke my ass. All I could do was laugh.

"Umm... is this your idea of a date? You got me at a warehouse? This better be good, Firm. This better be good."

"Ohhhh, I'm Firm now? Trust me, ma. You'll want to see what's on the other side of those doors. You strapped? I ain't up for torturing today."

Her head snapped back, but then a devious smile spread across her beautiful face.

"Always. Let's go!"

What more could you ask for? A gorgeous female that was a rider, didn't mind getting her hands dirty, and had more streams of income than a little bit. On top of that, she never let any of it go to her head; she was down to earth and humble as hell.

When we walked into the warehouse, three niggas from my team were posted throughout different areas, handling different things. It all looked legal to the untrained eye, considering they had on hard hats and safety vests, but what they were doing was anything but. I led Ki'Asia to the staircase that housed a room at the top. She gave me a skeptical look but followed behind me anyway.

Once I unlocked the door to the room and she entered, she looked back at me and her eyes lit up.

"Is that who I think it is? The one and only Mr. Andarius Cuthbertson, aka Dreek. How you get Dreek out of Andarius?" she questioned, smiling as she walked closer to him.

I had some of my men scoop Dreek up the night we killed Branden, not being the one to chance him coming after us again. I could have involved some of the members from her team, but I wanted to surprise her and also see her in action again. Something about the way she bust her guns that night at the dudes in the car, did it for me. Most of the females I'd dealt with were too scared to hold a gun, let alone shoot one.

Since the night we took him from his house, we hadn't given him anything other than bread and water. There was a bathroom in the room that he had free rein to use, and I wasn't the least bit worried about him trying to escape. I had three people on duty watching the warehouse at all times, alternating shifts, so him escaping wasn't happening.

"Bitch, fuck you! You can't do shit but wet my dick up," he said weakly.

Gun in hand, I walked up to him and slapped the shit out of him with the butt of the gun.

"Mind ya fucking manners, nigga. Fuck wrong wit' you!" I barked on his ass.

"Oh no, Firm. It's OK. You want me to get your little dick wet, right?" Ki'Asia said, removing his dick from his boxers. She went in her purse and put on a pair of latex gloves. *Who the fuck walks around with latex gloves in their purse?* What she pulled out next really fucked my head up. She squeezed a small amount of KY Jelly in her hand and started stroking this nigga's dick in front of me.

"Yo, ma. Chill the fuck out with that shit," I told her.

When she looked back at me, I swear it looked like her normal hazel colored eyes had turned black as coal.

"I need to get that dick nice and hard if I'ma suck it. Ain't that right, Dreek?" This nigga's stupid ass had the nerve to nod his head with a smile on his face. If he knew like I knew, he'd try to get the hell away from this crazy woman, because right now, I wasn't even sure what the hell she was capable of.

In less than a second, it seemed, Ki'Asia spit a blade from her mouth and sliced that nigga's shit down the middle. *I* felt his pain. His screams *mirrored* his pain. Ki'Asia, on the other hand, smiled widely, looking like the got damn Joker.

"There... Nice and wet. Now let's have some real fun. Dreek... why couldn't you come to me like a man and say you wanted in? Why did it have to come to this? I mean... you killed one of my men. I don't take shit like that lightly."

The craziest part of the whole scene was she sat there unfazed and was really waiting for the man to answer her.

"Dreeeeek, I don't wanna repeat myself. It's not gonna be preeeetttyyyyy," she sang. This girl was batshit crazy. I had to chuckle because I was damn near too scared to do anything else.

She sat impatiently waiting, tapping her heel against the concrete floor before finally releasing a sigh.

"Firm, he don't wanna talk to meeeee. Ohhhh, wait. I think I got something that'll make him talk."

She dug into that big suitcase/purse she had and pulled out her phone.

"Look, Dreek. There's your brother. Don't he look nice?" When she finished, "Firm, wanna see?" she turned around and asked, showing me her phone. Each picture she flipped through was a different body part, until finally, a video came on of someone placing all Branden's body parts on a gurney and sending it through the incinerator. *Damn. Burn in hell, Branden... literally!*

Her smile was gone as she faced Dreek again.

"You think this shit is a fucking game? I asked you a question. Why couldn't you come to me like a man and ask for what you wanted? My pretty ass coulda got killed the other night behind your non-shooting ass team!" she yelled, and her body started trembling.

"It-it-it wasn't sup-supposed to be like that. They were

supposed t-t-to take out your team and Firm and his team. It wasn't supposed to take place at any s-spot you were at. Only places your t-t-team be," he said.

"So why the fuck would you involve Sabria?" I asked him, sort of wishing Trapp was here to get some closure.

"That wa-wasn't on me. Branden wasn't supposed to kill her. He was only supposed to get close to her to find out y'all moves. That was something he did on his own. Said something about her digging into his information and finding out too much about him. I didn't authorize that," he said, finally able to talk through the pain.

"Why you wait until now to wanna strike against me? The shit that happened what your team was over a year ago," I had to ask.

"It's n-n-not me. Tu-Tuf..." His sentence trailed off, and the nigga passed out.

Before I could stop her, Ki'Asia pulled her gun and let off three shots to his head, close range.

"Damn, ma. I wanted to hear what he had to say."

"Well, dead men don't talk, so now you can't. This is what we need to do..."

For the next half hour, we devised a plan to get rid of Dreek's team and take over his areas. Considering his territories were widespread, we needed to place a decoy and fast.

Once we finished up in there, we walked back downstairs, and I told my men to clean up. Before we made it to the car, I stopped Ki'Asia by gently grabbing her waist and pulling her back to me.

"I don't know where you get that name Murda from, but that shit's dead. You getting ready to be Queen City's Finest, ma," I told her. She looked back at me and smiled, nodding her head.

"I like that. And by the way, this shirt was $405, the pants were $520, and..." She looked down at her heels. "Oh, they straight. But you owe me $925 for my outfit." She stuck her tongue out before pulling away from me, and all I could do was smile at her little pretty ass. Little did she know, she could have the world.

***

After I dropped her off to the apartment near the club to change clothes and I went home and did the same, I picked her back up a little after noon, and we headed to McCormick and Schmick's since she said she had a taste for seafood. Once we ate lunch, we decided to do a matinee, and of course, she would pick some girly shit, *Why Did I Get Married Too?* which ended up not being girly but not as good as the first one.

We ended the evening at my sister's house, which turned into a three-hour stay. Between my sisters and niece gushing over her, and that bomb ass meal Anise prepped, I was tired and ready to take my ass home.

Ki'Asia told me where her main house was, and after we said our goodbyes to my sisters and I tucked my niece in, we headed that way. On the drive over, she drifted off to sleep. I kept stealing glances at her while trying to focus on the road at the same time. She was just so beautiful to me. Her personality appealed to me more than anything. She was sweet and gentle as a person, but no-nonsense when it came to handling her business.

Half an hour later, we pulled up to her spot. I turned the car off and sat for a moment, still staring, listening to her light snores, before waking her up. When she saw where she was, she grabbed her purse while I walked around to open the door for her. Once we reached the door, she turned in my direction.

"Thank you for everything today, Tyleek. When the day started out, I didn't know what to think, but I truly enjoyed myself from sun up to sundown. But..." She put her head down, being bashful. That was something that bugged me out about her. The hardest female I knew, but at times, she was shy as hell. I lifted her chin up so she could look me in the eyes and tell me what she had to say.

"Talk, ma. Kill that shy shit," I told her.

"Umm... I'm not ready for the day to come to an end."

"Then it won't."

She cracked a little smile before turning around and unlocking the door. Once we walked in, it was nothing short of what I expected from someone of her caliber. From the color scheme to the modern décor, it screamed Queen.

After she locked the door and set the alarm, I followed behind as we made our way to the living room.

"Would you like something to drink? I got..." She trailed off as she walked to the kitchen and went through the fridge and then turned to look at something in the corner, which I assumed was a rack or stand of some sort. "...Heineken, Corona, Moscato, Goose, VSOP, Louis XIII—just pick something. Just about anything you want, I got," she said, and we both laughed.

"I'll take VSOP and Coke, ma."

"You can go through the DVD's and find something to watch. I'm burnt on girly movies, so don't try to pick anything for me!" she yelled from the kitchen.

I got up and looked at the entertainment center. I opened the doors to it but didn't see anything but crystal figurines, which let me know she switched her shit up frequently. I was getting ready to call out to her to ask where they were until I saw a sliding door in the wall on the side of the entertainment center. Sure enough, I slid the door open, and this girl had a damn walk-in closet with DVD's from ceiling to floor on both sides. She had movies I'd never even heard of and some I never knew were even on DVD.

"Damn," I said aloud while walking through. Of course, she had all the hood classics, so I settled on *Scarface*.

When I walked out, she was placing the two drinks in coasters on the coffee table.

"Don't start the movie without me. I'm going to run upstairs and take a quick shower and change into something more comfortable," she said before darting up the steps.

While waiting, I decided to look at a photo album that was somewhat hidden to the side of the entertainment center in a magazine rack. She had pictures of her and Da'Jon when they were little and living in New York. I saw more pictures of them with their father than with their mother, and the ones I did see with their mother was of them as a family with their father included. I saw where Ki'Asia got her hazel eyes from now, but aside from that, the dimples, and complexion, everything else was her mother. Her mother was a little dime piece herself—short and thick.

When I got to the last couple of pages, I saw pictures

from our high school days. There were some of her and Desiree and some of the other girls I knew Desiree to hang with more, and then the very one picture she and I had taken together, hugged up by the lockers. She and I were dressed alike with the big striped Hilfiger shirts. I remember buying us those shirts when she agreed to be my girl. The very last page almost knocked the wind out of me. She was hugged up with my uncle, Jackson.

"What the fuck?" I said louder than intended to.

"What the fuck, what?" she asked, rounding the corner.

"Yo, you used to deal with this nigga or something?" I questioned, showing her the picture. But I was about to say fuck it when I saw what she had on. The pink silk two-piece short pajama set left nothing to the imagination, I tell you that!

She looked at me with her brow raised before she burst out laughing.

"No, nosy. That's my supervisor at the law firm I work at as a paralegal. That was the day I was named Paralegal of the Year by Advocate."

"Wow... this a small ass world. Jackson is my uncle," I told her, and it was her time to be shocked.

"Who's Jackson?"

"My bad. You probably call him Mr. Williams. Jackson Brown Williams is the crazy nigga's name. My grandma gave him three last names," I said, and we both chuckled.

"Definitely interesting. Yeah... it definitely is a small world," she said before grabbing the DVD off the table and putting it in.

She sat down beside me, and I grabbed her by the shoulder to pull her closer. We both sat there watching the movie as if it were both of our first time seeing it. The movie was a scene away from being at the end, when they ran up in Al Pacino's mansion, and I heard her low snores. I looked down, and she was definitely knocked out.

Now see... had she been a chick I just wanted to smash, I would have taken advantage, and she would have woke up to a dick in her mouth. But I was feeling the fuck out of Ki, so that wasn't about to happen.

I turned the TV off with the remote and gently scooped her up in my arms. She wrapped her arms around my neck and snuggled closer in my chest. No lie, this girl was making me weak as fuck. When I got to her room, I slightly nudged the door with my foot and walked into a room fit for royalty. Her color scheme of pink, black, gold, and white was spread throughout her bedroom as well. I took note of it, assuming they were her favorite colors since they were also the colors she mostly rocked.

Once I placed her in the bed, covered her up, and kissed her forehead, I turned to leave.

"No, Tyleek, don't go," she said before I heard her snores again.

I scratched my head. It was going to be tough as hell to lay beside her and not fuck, but I did it anyway. I went through her bathroom and found the linen closet where she kept washcloths and towels, and took a shower, pleading with my mans to be on his best behavior. Once I got out and dried off, I got in the bed, free-balling. That night, I held her in my arms while she slept on my chest, and I vowed to protect her with everything in me.

Ki'Asia

When I woke up the next morning, I almost had a damn heart attack not remembering clearly at first the events from last night. I didn't admit it to Tyleek, but I wasn't a heavy drinker. Smoked like hell, but when I did drink, I'd get knocked on my ass quick. And the drink I fixed myself was pretty hefty, thinking I was going to end my drought and get Storm some action. Either Tyleek's dick was smaller than I remembered, or we didn't do anything, because Storm was still intact. With me not having sex in almost two years, trust and believe, she would have been sore as hell.

I looked over at him and wondered what life would be like with him by my side. Was this God's way of telling me that's why I couldn't get with anyone else, because I never got over my first? Or was I just reading too much into the time we'd been spending together? Whatever it was, I felt myself falling and fast.

I got up to handle my hygiene, and there was a little devil on my shoulder telling me to take a peek at what he was working with. Even though I gripped it a while back, I wanted to see it up close and personal. I slowly sat back on the bed and gently removed the cover, hoping he wasn't a light sleeper and would feel it. My ass should have kept the covers over him. *What the hell am I gon' do with that?* I questioned.

Tyleek had to be at least nine inches long and three inches thick. Then it had the nerve to curve. That shit was nothing like I remembered it being from high school. *Father, help me!* I slid the cover back and proceeded to my en-suite. After washing my face and brushing my teeth, I headed back in the bedroom with intentions of just lying there.

"Next time, don't peek. Do something about it," Tyleek's voice said, scaring the shit out of me.

"Shit! You tried to give me a heart attack! And do something about what?"

He removed the cover from his body, revealing the beautiful tool I'd stolen a glance at before going into the bathroom. I may have been a beast in the streets, but sexually, I was so inexperienced. I'd been with only two guys after him, and one of them had my mind so far gone, I thought I was going to have to end up killing his ass. From looking at what Tyleek was holding, I didn't want this to be another case of that.

Even with the inexperience and me being skeptical of getting caught up, seeing him in all his glory had my mouth watering... and I'd never had anything in my mouth other than food and drink.

"Don't be scared, ma. Remember, how you grabbed him through my jeans? Well the jeans gone, ma. Do ya thing," he said with a sexy smirk on his face.

You got this, Ki. Bitch, you better! It was a shame when your mind and vagina were both screaming encouragement. I slowly walked toward the side of the bed where Firm lay. Never one to be ashamed of my body, I seductively removed the thin pieces of fabric that covered it as he eyed my every move.

Sliding on top of him but making sure not to allow his little friend entrance, all inhibitions went out the window and I leaned over, taking control of his lips as his hands delicately gripped my behind. Suddenly, he flipped me over on my back, landing my legs in the perfect position on his shoulder.

"I'm getting ready to teach you how to let a man take the lead. It's OK to be in control, but with this..." He pointed between us both. "I'm in control," he said before his mouth greedily latched onto my pearl as if I was the sweetest thing he'd ever tasted.

Gently, he stuck one finger in my box while sucking on my clit, and I felt as if I was about to explode. I was really trying to hold back, but remember, it had been two years. When he inserted his thumb in my ass, that was it.

"Ahhhh, Tyleek, stooooop!" I screamed out, but ignoring me as I hoped he would, he continued his assault as my body convulsed. He removed his fingers and caught every bit of my juices in his mouth, not leaving any to get on the sheets. I thought he was finished, but his tongue replaced his fingers, alternating back and forth between both holes, causing another orgasm. Two orgasms in less than fifteen minutes; he'd definitely set a record.

Before my body had a chance to respond or recuperate, Tyleek had pressed both of my thighs down to the bed and slowly eased his way inside of me, making me gasp. Honestly, the pain was almost unbearable.

"Ssss... got damn, ma. This shit tight and wet as fuck," he groaned. Releasing my thighs, he leaned forward, sticking his tongue in my mouth, allowing me to taste the remnants of my juices. His mouth left mine, finding its way to my breasts where he gently sucked, licked, and bit on my nipples, showing each the same attention.

"Ahh, fuck," he moaned out again. For some reason, it didn't bother me that he hadn't strapped up; I trusted him that much, and that was a first for me.

The further he went in my box, the pain that I was experiencing was turning into pleasure, permitting my body to respond. Once I caught his rhythm, I began matching him stroke for stroke.

My muscle tightened around his dick, and the feeling caused both of us to scream out.

"Fiiiiirrrrmmmm, oh my God!" I yelled, tears rolling down my face from pure bliss. He was handling my body like it was made just for him. Abruptly, he stopped.

"Open your eyes, Ki," he said in a low voice. When I

opened them and stared into his eyes, I didn't see lust; all I saw was genuine love from this man.

Keeping eye contact, he started back grinding into me with slow strokes. Firm closed my legs together and held them up, and that's when all signs of being gentle went out the door.

"Ahh... oh shit... oh my God! I... can't... take... it!" I screamed out, but he continued going, making sure to keep eye contact. If I turned my head, he would use his free hand to turn it back in his direction. Looking him in the eyes was causing my juices to flow even more.

Once he let my legs down, he demanded me to turn over on my stomach. I did as he asked, and before I could get comfortable, he had my ass up in the air with his face buried deep between both my cheeks.

"Mm... mmm... aaaaggghhhhhh," I grunted, unable to take what he was doing to my body. I didn't even know it was possible to secrete from your ass, but he showed me. He was taking my body to heights I'd never imagined. When his tool slid back in me, he showed no mercy. From smacking my ass cheeks to pulling my hair and licking up and down my back, he worked my body better than any... well, the other two I'd been with.

"Right there, baby. I'm cumming... I'm cummiiiinnnng!" I screamed, followed by his grunts, as we both climaxed at the same time, his seeds swimming deep within me.

I was too spent to do anything. I couldn't move, Storm was crying, and yet I felt so alive. Firm got up and went to the bathroom where I heard the water running for the shower. When he came back into the room, he picked me up in his arms, carrying me to the shower.

Until the water turned cold, we fucked, washed, fucked, and washed again. As we lay in the bed with my head on his chest, Firm tilted my chin up to look at him.

"You know you mine now, right? That means I'm your lover, best friend, protector... I'm your king, ma. And trust me when I tell you, I got you. You hear me?"

I nodded my head, confirming I'd heard him before kissing his lips and falling asleep. Now I just had to get the one person's approval who meant more to me than life itself.

***

When I woke up, it was 2:10, and Firm was no longer laying under me. I was even more sore than I was before falling asleep. I rolled over and grabbed my phone off the nightstand and saw I had three text messages from Desiree, a missed phone call from her, and a text from Da'Jon. Desiree was excited about finishing her classes and coming home in time to get prepared for the grand opening. I was low-key excited my damn self. So much so, I'd forgotten to mention in to Firm. Where the heck was he at anyway? I checked my business phone and saw no text messages or missed calls, which was a good thing.

As I got up and headed to my walk-in closet to grab some sheets and my outfit for the day, I thought about how my father would feel with me, not only partnering with someone else, but mixing business with pleasure. He always told me the two didn't mix, but I wanted him to see things my way. I felt this was the best thing that could have happened. Which reminded me, I needed to call my aunt Chan and tell her to get word to my father to add Firm to his visiting list.

I could have reached out to my father on my own, through letter or phone, but I was always worried about the consequences of me contacting him on the phone and he'd end up facing consequences that caused his privileges to be snatched from him. And doing it through letter would just take too long, and I needed him and Firm to meet ASAP.

After the sheets were changed, I took another shower, brushed my teeth again, got dressed, and headed down the steps.

"Now ya food cold as shit," Firm said as he placed a kiss on my forehead.

"Aww... I didn't know you were cooking. How did you know I was up?" I asked, noticing he had on a different outfit.

"I heard you moving around upstairs and decided to fix you some lunch. And before you ask, I grabbed your keys and went home to change. Now sit down while I warm up ya food," he said, and I didn't ask any questions.

A few minutes later, he brought me a plate of salmon with wild rice and salad.

"Did you go to sleep with me? When did you have time to prepare all this and go change clothes?" I questioned.

"Nah, I watched you sleep for a few minutes, and then I dipped out."

He sat across from me at the table, but before we could bless the food and eat, his phone started vibrating. He looked at the screen, chuckled, then handed the phone to me.

"Handle that," was all he said, and I noticed the name flashing on the screen said 'Carpet Muncher.' I laughed out loud before accepting the call.

"Hellooooo?"

"Oh, I'm sorry. I think I have the wrong number," the voice on the other end said.

"Oh, no. Tricie, is it? You have the right number, just the wrong man and at the wrong time. He's taken, boo. I'd advise you to move on, OK?" I said, remembering the situation and him saying her name the night I called him.

"Can I please just speak to Tyleek? I just want him to know I'm sorry. He can't just throw away two years and move on like everything is OK," she replied, snapping when she said the last part.

"I warned you," I said and ended the call.

Firm sat across the table, looking at me, and shook his head.

"She ain't gon' stop calling. Bitch gon' make me change my—"

Glass shattering and shots being fired halted his conversation. He basically jumped over the table and pushed me to the ground, shielding my body.

"What the fuck!" he yelled out.

I could only think of two things that could have happened, and one of them better not had been the issue, or bodies from my own team would be dropping.

Once the gunfire stopped, I moved to get up, and Firm looked at me like he was getting ready to take my head off my shoulders.

"Stay the fuck down, and don't get up until I tell you to!" he barked. Had he been anyone else, we would have been going toe to toe for talking to me like that, but I remembered when he said I had to let him lead. It may have been in a passion-filled moment, but I was listening.

He stood up and removed his gun from under the table, which shocked the hell out of me, checked the clip, and made his way to the door. He looked out the window first... well, what was left of the window, then opened the door.

"Damn," he said, and I knew he had to have been talking about either damage to the exterior of the home or his car. I said his because mine was the least thing I was worried about. It was bulletproof and like a home away from home with the customized components I had added to it.

He closed the door and walked back in, sighing heavily.

"Can I get up now, master?" I sarcastically asked.

Firm gave me a look that said 'cut the shit,' and I chuckled inwardly.

"Get up and tell me what's going on. Who the hell would be shooting up ya shit?"

Like I said, I only had two thoughts. "Well, it ain't many possibilities. Either you were being followed, or someone on my team, Desiree, Da'Jon, or my moms leaked my info. The last three is some very unlikely possibilities, and when I say someone on my team, it can only be the heads of each team because they're the only ones that know where I lay my head."

He sat there in deep thought, allowing what I said to soak in. "Nah, ma. Ain't nobody follow me, bet that. I'm too careful for that shit. Hit ya team up and call a meeting for this evening," Firm said before walking off and heading up the steps. I was going to have to get used to letting someone else lead, because I never liked to be told what to do.

***

On our way to Firm's warehouse, I sent my aunt Chan a text, while I remembered, to tell my dad to add Tyleek Ditmas to his visitation list. I told Firm about the grand opening of the club that was scheduled in the next upcoming month, and he wanted to hire extra security. He said he'd been hearing about it on the radio but didn't put two and two together that it was my club they were talking about. In addition, he wanted the name of the deejay, bartenders, cooks, and everyone else who was going to be in attendance that had access to inside the club.

When we pulled up to the warehouse, Firm parked and cut off the ignition then turned to face me.

"Look... I'm not trying to run shit. Trust me when I tell you that. I like the way you handle ya business, and I'll never take that from you. I don't want no weak ass female in my corner anyway, and you've proven to be far beyond that.

But what you need to do is tone it down on this end. No one knows Murda. Let it stay that way. I'm front and center and you play the back. All anyone knows about Ki'Asia is that she is a queen... and she's Queen City's Finest, remember that," he stated with authority.

As opposed to getting mad, I took it all in, because what he was saying made sense. With him being the face and me playing the background, I still had my control but didn't have to worry about getting my hands dirty to do it.

"Yes, daddy," I replied as I reached over, placing a kiss to his lips, in which he responded by grabbing the back of my head and sticking his tongue down my throat.

"Keep it up with that daddy shit if you want to." He released his hold on the back of my neck, then hopped out the car and came to open the door for me.

When we got in the warehouse, I followed Firm through the warehouse to what I thought was going to be an exit but ended up being a big ass conference room with vending and drink machines. There were four 8-seater conference tables. The heads of my team occupied one table, minus Biggz, and Trapp and some other guy I'd never seen sat at one of the other tables.

"Why are your guys here?" I stood on my tiptoes and pulled Firm's head down to whisper to him.

He looked at me through slits before he began addressing my men.

"Queen, have a seat," he instructed me.

"Excuse me?"

"I said have a fucking seat!" he barked, and two of my men pulled pistols which caused Trapp and the other guy to draw theirs. I didn't know what the fuck was going on, but I didn't like the shit at all.

He stared me in the eyes, daring me to blink. I didn't know whether it was because I felt some type of hurt or what, but I did end up blinking. Once I did, a tear fell down my cheek, and I could see the hurt in his eyes, but he didn't allow it to cause him to comfort me.

I sat down in the chair, conflicted. Now I saw why my daddy told me to never mix business with pleasure. Feelings got in the way and caused you to make irrational decisions which were not generally made without feelings being involved. Point taken.

"Pop, Preme, put your guns down." They both looked at him and he threw his hand in the air and slowly brought it down which made them lower their guns. I looked at both of them like they were crazy as hell. I didn't command them to do a damn thing.

"I don't know what the fu—" The look Firm gave me prevented me from speaking further. He walked over in my direction and bent down to whisper in my ear.

"Let… me… lead," he said. I looked up at him and then looked at my brother Pop. I also turned to look at Trapp along with every head of my team, and all of them spoke their confirmation through eye contact or with a nod of the head. Feeling somewhat defeated, I sat back in my chair, pouting, and let him lead.

"Now that I have y'all attention, somebody..." He looked in the eyes of every member on my team. "...has some explaining to do. Earlier today, Ki's house was shot up. From my understanding, the only people that knows where she lives is in this room, aside from three other people. So what's good? Talk to me?" Tyleek said as he took a seat.

"What the fuck you mean somebody shot up my sister's house? No disrespect, son, but Ki'Asia, that's some shit you should have called and told me immediately," my brother Pop said, and I could tell he was mad as hell, because his light skin complexion was anything but at the moment. They never felt the need to put detail on my house because no one ever knew where it was, so I knew he was feeling like shit right now.

Before I could answer, Tyleek spoke up.

"Pop... Preme... let me holla at y'all for a minute," Tyleek said, walking out into the warehouse without waiting for a response from either of them.

"Yo, I like son, but word is bond, he ain't the fuckin' boss of me, and you better let him know that shit. I don't give a damn if you is fuckin' him," Pop said which caused me to jump up out my seat.

"Nigga, you better remember who the fuck you talkin' to, because right now, I'm starting to think yo' ass is looking real suspect. And whether I'm fuckin' him or not ain't got a damn thing to do with somebody shootin' up my spot, nigga. You better pipe that shit down, 'cause brother or not, I'll end ya life and send you back to NY to my godfather in an urn. Try me, nigga."

Pop had me fucked all the way up. I couldn't even believe he came at me like that. Then he had the audacity to look like he really was going to attempt to do something until Preme grabbed him by the arm.

"You buggin' the fuck out, Pop. Come on. You know everybody in this bitch will light ya ass up behind baby girl. It's a suicide mission, son."

Pop glared at me before he snatched away from Preme and headed out the door to go talk to Tyleek.

I sat back down, trying so hard not to cry. Da'Jon may have been my only biological brother, but Pop and I were raised together since the crib. For him to come off on me like that really hurt me and pissed me off at the same time.

Trapp came over and threw his arm around me.

"So, sis. Check this out. I know this might be the wrong time to ask this, but you bonin' my boy for real?"

I looked at him and he was dead ass serious. I couldn't do anything but burst out laughing. Leave it to this dude to change up my mood.

"Nunya business, little boy," I replied as I mushed him.

Trapp introduced me to the other dude, whose named I learned was Stab, and we all sat around talking until Tyleek, Pop, and Preme came back in.

Pop walked over to me and bent down and kissed me on the forehead.

"My bad, sis. I apologize. You know you my heart, and I was hurt that you ain't come to a nigga to let me know what was going on, but ya man explained to me.

You got a real one, sis. Good looks, baby girl."

I nodded my head and smiled so he would know there was no hard feelings, but I was still mad at his little peanut head ass.

Chapter 7

"A queen never steps off her throne to address a peasant."

Firm

Two months later

After the meeting at the warehouse that night, Ki'Asia and I got into a little bit of an argument and I sent her home in her feelings. I was feeling the hell out of baby girl and was on the brink of telling her I loved her because, shit, it was the damn truth, but she really needed to learn how to let a nigga lead. I understood wholeheartedly that she was used to running things the way she saw fit, but I honestly didn't think everyone on her team was keeping it one hundred. I couldn't point my finger at who, but some shit wasn't adding up.

For example, all of the heads were supposed to be at the meeting, yet Biggz was missing. Now I knew she told me Biggz was back and forth from here to NY, but at that moment, he was there, so where the fuck was he? And then Trapp told me about the little slick ass comment Pop made to her when I left out the room, which I should have been paying more attention to. I knew Pop was Biggz's son, so was it possible that they could have been working together to take not only her down but me as well? Was this bigger than Dreek? I had all kinds of thoughts running through my mind, but as I told them in the meeting, we were getting ready to bring both teams together and eliminate the body since the head—that we knew of—was gone. It would take a while, but it would be done.

That Wednesday once Desiree made it into town, we all met up at the club for Ki'Asia to introduce all of the staff, and from there, I took over. And when I say took over, I meant took over. I changed the grand opening date, which pissed her slam the fuck off, but I'd be damned if I gave niggas a way to get at me by bringing her down. I wanted the problem with Dreek's team solved before her grand opening, and I made sure of it. And now, the night had finally come. Little did she know, it was going to be one for the books. I had pulled out all the stops for my baby's grand opening to be a success. She didn't know I had been working with Desiree and Da'Jon on certain things, but her mind was definitely going to be blown.

This morning, I had taken her to meet my pops for the first time ever. He'd talked to her on the phone here and there and had heard about her through Anise and Taysia but had never met her. Let's just say Ki'Asia's charm and beauty affected young and old. He was absolutely infatuated with her, and it was obvious in the way he stared, kept kissing her hand, and hung on to her every word.

Before we left out the door, he pulled me back and asked if he could have a word with me alone and gave Ki'Asia a hug and kiss to the cheek and told her she was his daughter-in-law. And that's exactly what he told me when she left and he and I were alone: to make her the mother of my child and his daughter-in-law.

I looked at the time and realized it was two hours before showtime. Right before I went to jump in the shower, my cell started ringing, and from the ringtone, I knew it was someone from my team.

"Speak to me," I answered when I noticed it was Stab.

"It's done," he said and disconnected the call.

For the past two months, he and those up under him were responsible for going to Salisbury, Winston, and Greensboro and shutting down Dreek's spots there, killing everything moving and taking all product. I wanted everything to be done in chorus, but evidently, Dreek was in the process of moving his blocks around before his untimely demise, so I couldn't touch the crew he had in High Point at all. I was more so hoping them niggas would have just bowed out without their leader, but only time would tell if that shit happened, especially with everyone else being wiped off the face of the earth.

I ran up the steps and jumped in the shower, thinking about how happy Ki'Asia was going to be tonight. The love she received from this city was already amazing, and tonight would be no different. Once I stepped out the shower, dried off, and brushed my teeth, I walked nude into the closet and grabbed the outfit I had chosen for tonight. Knowing Ki'Asia was wearing all white, I wanted to match her fly and keep it simple at the same time, so I chose a white Dolce and Gabbana button-up with the slacks and moccasins. I kept my jewelry light with a simple Rolex and platinum Cuban with the Jesus piece on my neck. By no means was I a flashy nigga, and that was one of the things I admired about Ki'Asia; she was even less flashy than I was. I grabbed my keys and shot the driver a text and was on my way.

When I pulled up to the club, just like I thought, there was a line wrapped around the corner. The sign immediately drew you in, with the bright pink letters ***Touch of Class Nightclub***. The red carpet was laid out at the entrance of the double doors, just like I'd requested, but the only person allowed to walk the entire full length of the red carpet was Ki'Asia. There were roped-off sections with two lines from either side of the entrance for the patrons to enter.

I had security tight as hell considering what took place at Ki'Asia's house a couple months back. Unbeknownst to her, security was blended in the crowd on the inside as well as shooters positioned outside waiting for anything to jump off. I was not putting my girl's life in the hands of her team until I figured out who could be trusted. However, Da'Jon and Trapp worked together with me on this to make sure everything went smoothly, and of course, I had my men on it as well.

After I dapped up the bouncer and walked in, I was shocked to say the least, so I knew Ki would be in awe at the way things had turned out. I didn't know how the people outside waiting were going to get in, because the club was almost at capacity. I expected a crowd, but this exceeded my expectations, and I knew it would surpass hers. As good as this was, it was also not the best situation. Too many people and not enough eyes watching meant that anything could jump off. I looked around to make sure that everybody I had positioned were in place and counted a total of fifteen of my men.

I saw Desiree at the bar and headed in her direction.

"What's up, girl?" I said over the music. "What you doing behind the bar instead of up in VIP?"

"What's good, bruh! I was waiting for the woman of the hour, but since you're here, I guess I can go on up.

Plus, Trapp's thirsty ass ain't stopped hitting on me since he got here. You better get ya boy 'fore I catch a body," she said, and I laughed.

When Trapp saw Desiree, real shit, the nigga was drooling. Trapp was a tall ass nigga like me, and Desiree stood around five ten, but she still had to look up at Trapp a little bit. She had a shape on her and was a pretty ass girl, with a mocha complexion, shoulder-length hair, and slanted eyes. But let Trapp tell it, she was the baddest thing he'd ever seen in his life. I doubt she'd give Trapp a chance because he was a year younger than her, but on the real, Trapp was well beyond his years. I could see that being a good look.

Once she stepped from behind the bar, we headed up to the VIP section, with me dapping a few people up along the way, and her speaking to and giving hugs to some people she said she knew from school or around the way. Just like she said, as soon as we entered the VIP section, Trapp was on her like white on rice.

"Aight, niggas. Y'all see that one right there? That's wifey. Eyes, hands, everything off, or the shits'll be removed for you. Aight? Bet. Now that we have an understanding, come here, wife," he said, causing the entire section to laugh, including Desiree.

"Boy, yo' young ass wouldn't know what to do with me. Don't get it twisted. I'd be done messed around and had *you* climbing the walls!"

"Shit! Don't threaten me with a good time, wit' yo' fine self!" Trapp yelled, shaking his head and licking his lips.

She talked that shit, but her ass was blushing as she walked right over there and sat beside him. On the real, something was going on with those two. I didn't give a damn what her mouth said.

I sat on a couch by myself, waiting for the queen to arrive. Each of the tables had a bottle of Ace, Rosé, or Louis, so I grabbed a bottle of Ace and poured me a glass. A few minutes went by before my boy Yayo finally made an appearance. Each of the heads and a few of the foot soldiers were invited to the VIP section from both teams. The majority of my foot soldiers were either mingling in the crowd or outside, as well as the few more Da'Jon and

Trapp recruited. Speaking of Da'Jon, I didn't see him.

"Yo, Desiree, Trapp, where Jon at!" I yelled out over the music. The DJ was doing his damn thing, and the crowd was hyped as hell.

"Oh shit. He said he was going to be... shit, there he go right there," Trapp pointed, and Da'Jon was headed up to the VIP area with a bad little shorty on his arm. Only thing was, she looked real familiar. I mean like 'red flag' familiar. I waited until they got a little closer to see if I could figure out where I knew her from.

Once he got up to the section, he immediately made an introduction.

"What's up, y'all. This my girl, Erica. Erica, this is..." He went around telling her everyone's name, but for some reason, she zoned in on me. I mean, she was cordial to everyone else and smiled, but once he made the introduction to me, she started speaking. Her name didn't register to me, and once she was up on me, she looked even more familiar, and her striking up a conversation made it even more suspicious.

"So you're Firm. How are you?" she asked, reaching

her hand out. I looked down at her hand and up at Trapp. He shrugged his shoulders.

"You know me, ma?"

She reached her hand up, acting like she was pushing a piece of imaginary out of place hair behind her ear, playing it off, and said, "I don't know you personally, but who doesn't know Firm. You're the man in these streets, as if you didn't know."

I picked up my glass and eyed her over the rim. This bitch screamed fake, and I was going to find out what the deal was with her. Da'Jon didn't peg me for the stupid nigga type, but pussy made you lose sight of reasoning sometimes, and that may have been the case in this situation.

"Oh... aight. Well nice meeting you," I said as I set my glass down and rose from my seat. I needed to use the bathroom real quick.

I headed to the bathroom to handle my business. As I washed my hands, I couldn't get ole girl off my mind. I never forgot a face, and hers was for damn sure one I had seen. I hated remembering something but not being able recall where or why I was remembering it. Then it hit me. Shorty's name for damn sure wasn't Erica; it was Ulysess, and she was dating Dreek when we were in high school. I knew that bitch looked familiar. And I should know because she was one of the few I fucked after I got out of school, with her loose ass pussy.

Once I wiped my hands off, opened the door, and rounded the corner, ready to go confront this bitch, whose face was I staring in? None other than Tricie's. And I had to admit, pussy licker looked like she had stepped off a ghetto runway. She was giving these females a run for their money, no doubt.

Involuntarily, my dick bricked up. At the end of the day, I was still a man, and I still had eyes, and I never said Tricie wasn't a beautiful girl. She had on a blue two-piece skirt set. The shirt was a halter style shirt and stopped right up under those big ass breasts, showing off her flat ass stomach. The skirt left nothing to the imagination. Tricie was a thick ass girl, but she was perfectly proportioned, meaning she was all tits, ass, hips, and thighs with no waist at all. I mean none. Her body looked like she lived in a gym. Ate, shit, and breathed it.

But what I heard and saw next put Tricie's ass to shame.

"And the queen has entered the building, y'all. Touch of Class, give it up for Queen City's Finest, Ms. Ki'Asiaaaaa," the deejay announced, which was what I told him to make sure he called out when she came in, and when I turned and looked in the direction of the entrance, my heart stopped. I knew Ki'Asia was fine as fuck, of course, but tonight, she went all out, and as if my dick wasn't hard enough, it started pointing directly at her ass.

She stood at the entrance in a short white strapless dress with the sides cut out, hugging every curve of her slim thick body. Her long hair was pulled up in a ponytail with curls hanging to the left, and a tiara adorned her head. The iced-out crown sitting on the platinum Cuban link I bought her sat right above her cleavage, showing off my best friends, the matching bracelet was on her wrist, and the pendant drop crown earrings were hanging from her ears. How the hell she was able to walk in them damn silver six-inch heels was beyond me, but there she stood with them on her feet. The biggest smile graced her face when our eyes met, and it was as if we were the only two in the room. I swear this girl was making me the softest nigga on earth.

Just as I took a step in her direction, I felt a hand gently grab my arm. When I turned and saw it was Tricie, my whole facial expression changed. For a moment, I forgot that I had just been looking at her. Hell, I almost forgot who the hell she was. Then all of a sudden, I heard from above me, “this bitch got me fucked up.” Coming full speed down the steps from the VIP was Desiree with Trapp, Da’Jon, Pop, Raquan, Yayo, and Preme right behind her. I knew if I didn’t get this situation under control, shit was getting ready to get real.

Ki'Asia

I looked myself over in the mirror, and once I was satisfied with my appearance, I grabbed my clutch, set my alarm, and headed out the door. What awaited me on the other side of the door was nothing short of breathtaking. Tyleek had really went all out. There, on the curb, sat a pink Hummer with 'Queen City's Finest' written on the side in white cursive letters. A smile a mile wide graced my face.

Once I made it to the truck, the driver opened the back door, reached his hand out, and assisted me in the back seat. There were two dozen white roses laying on the seat with a note attached.

Tonight is all about you, so kick back, relax, and enjoy the ride to your grand opening. I know I never told you face to face, but I love you, Ki'Asia Synese Barron. Wishing you much success.

Your man, Tyleek

He didn't have to tell me something that I could look in his eyes and see so easily. *Tyleek has loved me since we were in high school, even though he didn't know it back then.* I giggled at the thought, knowing he nor I could truly process the emotions we felt when we were teenagers. I was just glad we were able to reconnect and pick up like we never left off.

When we reached the street of the club, I was a little confused because, although the parking lot was overfilled and the streets surrounding had cars lined up everywhere, people were walking off.

"What the hell is going on?" I said aloud. Once the car came to a stop, I grabbed my clutch and jumped out, not giving the driver a chance to open the door. I immediately stopped at the red carpet when photographers started snapping pictures left and right. Although I was upset thinking the worst, I still had to put on my best face, knowing this was going to be in the newspapers first thing Monday morning, if not tomorrow.

As soon as the flashing of the cameras slowed down, I did a prissy girl walk with a fake smile plastered on my face, up to the bouncer.

"Why the fuck are people leaving my club, Irvin?"

“Boss lady... you’ll see.”

When he opened the doors, my mouth dropped. The club was in full swing, and the DJ was blasting Busta Rhymes’ “Touch It.” I knew I was close to being shut down because it was over capacity. I looked over at him and started grinning like the damn Cheshire cat.

“See, I told you. You was ready to whip my ass,” he said, and I could only laugh.

I walked through the doors and I heard “And the queen has entered the building, y’all. Touch of Class, give it up for Queen City’s Finest, Ms. Ki’Asiaaaaa!”

Everyone started screaming, whistling, clapping, and just making a bunch of noise. I looked around the club, and I promise if I didn’t want to ruin the little bit of makeup I did have on, I would have been in tears. When I say your girl brought the city out, she brought the city out.

I was also in awe at how amazing whoever Tyleek had to decorate, hooked it up. This was my dream, and it really was coming to life right in front of my eyes. I looked up in the VIP section that I knew my family and friends were supposed to be seated and saw all my loved ones except for Walt and my mother, who I knew were going to be late. She'd texted me prior to me leaving the house. I also didn't see Tyleek which was strange. But when I looked straight ahead, there he was, staring at me at me as if I were the only person that existed in his world. It caused me to smile ever so brightly.

We began to walk toward each other, but some female grabbed his arm. This definitely wasn't the shit I needed tonight. Oh, not tonight. I didn't let it slow my strides one bit. I kept moving toward my man like the bad chick I knew I was.

Before I could make it to him, Desiree was already over there, all up in shorty's face. Never one to hate on a beautiful woman, I'd admit just that, she was beautiful. Even with that being said, I wanted to know who she was.

I walked up on Tyleek, since his attention was evidently not on them and on me, stood on my tiptoes, wrapped my arms around his neck, and kissed *my* man.

"Ahhh, shit. Don't tell me the king of Queen City is with the queen? Damn, Firm. I see you, my nigga!"

As I wiped the lip gloss from his lips, he threw up his

hand to acknowledge the DJ before we turned around to the little situation on the side of us.

"So what's going on here?" I questioned.

"Same shit I wanna know," Desiree said, causing me to smirk.

"Who are you?" the girl asked, and I immediately caught on to the voice.

"Ohhhh, Tricie. Tricie, Tricie, Tricie… what a damn shame. Didn't I tell you when you called my man's phone that he was taken and that was my *only* warning to you?" I threw my hand on my hip in real ghetto girl fashion. I was getting ready to get a kick out of this.

"And didn't I tell you that I wanted to speak to Tyleek!" she yelled, coming closer to me, causing my eyes to widen and a big ass grin to form on my face.

"Pump ya brakes, munchie. You'll be dead before you can even lift ya arm to swing," Trapp said, causing me to laugh and Tyleek to shake his head.

Tyleek grabbed me by my waist and we proceeded to walk away until this bitch yelled out, "I said I needed to talk to you, Tyleek. I'm pregnant!"

My eyes rolled in the top of my head and I could feel my anger rising. *Calm down. It's your grand opening. It's about you. Make your father proud.*

I removed Tyleek's hand from my waist and turned back around before he could stop me. I knew my eyes had turned black because of the look of pure terror on her face.

I got close enough to her where she could smell what I had for breakfast emanating from my breath if she sniffed hard enough.

"I'd suggest you get rid of it, or I'll do it for you. I will literally stick my hand so far up your vagina and snatch that baby the fuck out of you, and then twist your uterus in all kinds of little funny ass directions, disabling you to ever have kids. Bitch, try me if you want to," I whispered in her ear then tapped her cheek. "Nice outfit by the way. Rainbow?" I laughed before walking off, headed up to VIP.

By the time I made it to the VIP area, my eye color had returned to normal, and it was like nothing had ever happened.

"You good, ma?" Tyleek questioned, sitting beside me.

I got up and sat on his lap.

"Of course. Why wouldn't I be? Look around. This is a freaking success, babe. Thank you soooo much!" I screamed, kissing all over his face. I knew he was probably wondering why I didn't let what happened faze me. It was because this wasn't the time or place. I would address the situation at a later time, but tonight was all about me and my success.

Tyleek, Desiree, and Da'Jon did a toast, and that's when I noticed the chick Da'Jon had with him.

"Who is that girl with Da'Jon, and why the hell does she look so familiar?" I whispered to Tyleek.

"Damn, I almost forgot. Yo, Jon, let me holler at you for a second!"

I saw Da'Jon bend down to kiss the girl's forehead before he trotted over in our direction. I kept squinting my eyes because I knew I'd seen this damn girl before.

"Before either of you start, yeah, that's Dreek's ole lady. She was actually still dating the nigga. Shorty a straight up ho, though, so I been hitting that since the nigga... disappeared. I'm trying to get some info out of her since she so loose with the lips, and if she doesn't have any info... I'd hate to lose those lips. And oh my gawd is she loose with those lips," he said, eyes rolling up in his head.

I popped him on the back as all of us burst out laughing.

"That's what's up, though. I thought you was losing ya mind or had done got pussy whipped, because I knew shorty was out there. And her name ain't no damn Erica either," Tyleek said.

"Sure ain't. I remember her now. That's Ulaho. That's what we called her in school," I added.

Before anyone could say anything else, my mother and Walt walked into the VIP section. For some reason, I got nervous. I didn't know why I let tonight be the night I introduced her to Tyleek, knowing how her ass was, but I figured since we were in public, she'd act like she had some sense.

Da'Jon and I both stood to greet her.

"Hi, Mommy," I said, kissing her cheek and giving her a hug.

"Sweetie, you look breathtaking... and getting thick as hell. Oh my goodness. And who is this young man? Has to be the infamous Tyleek I've been hearing about for the past few months," she said, looking behind me at Tyleek as he stood.

"Yes, Mommy, I would like you to meet my boyfriend, Tyleek. Tyleek, this is my mother, Maureen, and my stepfather, Walt," I said, introducing them both.

"Nice to meet you." He repeated the same gesture as I, hugging my mother and giving her a kiss on the cheek, and giving Walt a firm handshake.

For the rest of the night, everything was smooth sailing. Anise and Taysia even swung by. I was ecstatic that my grand opening was a success and I was able to share it with the people I loved the most. We danced, drank, and turned the fuck up all night!

***

I woke up the next morning to a sore Storm and a hangover from hell. Well, the next afternoon, I should say.

"Good afternoon, sleeping beauty," Tyleek said as he kissed my forehead.

"Hey, babe. What are you still doing in the bed? I

know you don't sleep in this late." I had to get up out his face because I smelled my breath, so I knew he did.

I hopped up out the bed before he could answer and went to the bathroom. After peeing, washing my hands, and turning on the shower, I peeked out the bathroom door, and of course he was undressing, making his way to the bathroom with me.

A smile graced my face as I thought about last night. Even after my mother and Walt got there, we all continued to enjoy ourselves. My mother and Walt took a liking to Tyleek, and I was pleased. I really didn't think she would be so receptive to me getting involved with someone that was in the game, but she even went as far as inviting us to dinner at her house next weekend, which was surprising considering our relationship.

Then I remembered Ms. Tricie. Oh, Ms. Motherfuckin' Tricie. Little did she know, I had some shit planned for her ass. As soon as I stepped in the shower, Tyleek was right behind me, and of course, now was the best time for me to bring up the topic of the carpet munchin' supposed baby mama.

I turned around to face him. “So, Firm... let me ask you a question real quick.”

“Ah shit. If you calling me Firm, it’s either business related—meaning some shit you wanna boss up on—or it’s some bullshit. Either or, I’m not up for it, Ki,” he said, and I scrunched up my face because right now, what was coming out of his mouth was straight shit.

“Your ex-girlfriend coming to my grand opening and screaming out she’s pregnant by you, is bullshit?” I questioned with a raised brow.

He looked at me with the ‘are you serious’ face before he burst out laughing.

“Look, ma,” he said, grabbing me around my waist, and like mush, I melted in his arms. This man has been my weakness for years, and time didn’t change that.

“There’s no way in hell Tricie can be pregnant by me. For one, and I know niggas say this all the time, but I never ran up in shorty without a condom. Now, you might find that hard to believe considering I don’t use condoms with you, but that’s because what me and you have is real. I told you, Tricie never had me.

For two, she stayed on her knees more than she stayed taking the dick. She couldn't handle it. She'd mastered sucking some dick now, don't get me wrong, but when it came to fuckin', her ass would run before I could get a nut, so even with a condom on, I usually ended up jacking my nut out or letting her suck it out.

Tricie said that shit to get a reaction out of you, and I'm glad the shit didn't work," he told me.

Whereas most females wouldn't have believed a word their man said about another female claiming they were pregnant, or they would have kept it in the back of their mind, I did neither. Tyleek had no reason to lie because, for one, Tricie was before me, and for two, I'm pretty sure he knew that she was going to get her little ass whipped after that stunt she pulled last night. One thing I didn't tolerate was ratchetness in public, and she was being straight disrespectful. But a queen never stepped off her throne to act like a peasant, so the reaction she expected wasn't the one she got.

I wrapped my arms around his neck as he lifted me up around his waist. I could not get enough of this man.

Since he and I had started having sex, I swear I wanted him any and everywhere.

"Ms. Ki'Asia Barron, you know I love you, right?"

I blushed, burying my head in his shoulder before looking back up into his face.

"I love you too, Tyleek. Always have."

"And you know one of these days, I'm giving you my last name, right? I don't give a fuck that we haven't been together long. Hell, I never even officially asked you to be mine—I told you you were mine, and I meant that shit. I knew from the moment I saw you again that first night in the funeral home, I wasn't going to let you out of my sight again. You complete me, babe. You the female version of me, and I need that in my life, feel me?" he said, and I saw the truthfulness in his eyes from the words he spoke.

I was about to shed a tear or two or three, but I just nodded my head up and down. He kissed me passionately on the lips before we washed each other off.

After getting out the shower, it seemed like we weren't dressed for more than two minutes before the doorbell rang.

"You expecting someone?" he asked, and I shook my head no. I glanced at my phone and Rock, one of the dudes that was guarding my house, had sent a text saying Desiree.

"It's Desiree, babe."

Tyleek ran down the steps to get the door while I placed my hair up in a high ponytail on top of my head. It had sweated out and was stringy yet thick from all the dancing I was doing last night, and I didn't feel like being bothered with it.

When I made it down the steps, Desiree was sitting on the couch, and Trapp and Tyleek were in the kitchen.

"What's good, sis?" Trapp asked as he looked at me and smiled.

I looked back and forth from him to Desiree. I swear I started to go back up the steps and come back down again, because I knew these two didn't come here together. Nah, that couldn't be it.

"Heyyyy, bruh. Umm... bitch..." I really had to pause and think about the question before I asked it. "Did you and Trapp come here together?" I questioned her.

She looked at me with wide eyes before they squinted, and she fell out laughing. I plopped down on the couch beside her and hollered.

"Girl, you letting Trapp's young ass dig in them guts!"

"Don't try and play me, sis! I ain't but a year behind y'all, shit!" Trapp yelled from the kitchen. I was too through. I could see it working out though. Trapp wasn't a nigga that stayed chasing behind pussy, so he was a good look for Desiree. She needed somebody to tame that ass, and even though Trapp joked a lot, Tyleek told me he had another side to him. I couldn't see him letting Desiree just run wild, regardless of the fact he was damn near obsessed with her.

I was getting ready to clown her ass some more, but a phone call was coming through on my line. When I looked at the screen, I saw it was my aunt Chan.

"Hey, Aunty!" I yelled into the phone, happy to hear from her.

"What's up, girl! I'm sorry I couldn't make it down

there for your grand opening, but don't worry. When I see you this week, I got a little surprise for you," she said.

Now I was confused. *See me this week?*

"Auntie, I wasn't coming up until Daddy let me know that Tyleek had been approved for visits," I informed her.

"Well then I guess I'll be seeing you and this Mr. Tyleek this weekend then," my daddy said, and I wanted to cry.

When I say I was a straight-up daddy's girl, even at the age of twenty-two, that's exactly what I was. My daddy was my world.

"Hi, Daddy! I miss you!" I damn near squealed.

"I miss you, too, princess. I can't wait to see you. And I've been hearing good things, baby. I'm proud of you," he said, and it caused me to smile widely. One of the things I lived for in life was to make my daddy proud, and so far, I had done just that with flying colors.

"I can't talk long, princess, but I want y'all to take a flight up and be here to see me Saturday, OK?"

"Yes, Daddy. I love you."

"I love you, too, princess. I'll see you then. Sis, get at

me. One," he said.

I looked down at my screen and saw that my aunt was still on the line.

"Auntie, you still there?"

"Yeah, I'm here. I want you to come up here a couple days earlier. You and Tyleek can stay with me. Get somebody to cover shit down there. We need to talk, Poot," she told me, calling me by the name she'd been calling me ever since I was a child.

"OK. I'm booking our flights now. I'll hit you up with the info. I love you," I told her, not liking how she sounded.

"I love you, too. Y'all be safe," she replied and disconnected the call.

I stared at my phone in my hand for a good minute.

"Everything straight, babe?" Tyleek asked as he walked into the living room.

"Yes, babe. We're headed to New York!" I yelled, a little too excited.

"Oh word? That's what's up. Ah shit, I get to meet the infamous Divine. I'm 'bout scared as—"

“The fuck!” Trapp yelled from the kitchen as he banged his hand down on the counter. He walked into the living room shaking his head. “Yo, Firm... sis... they killed Preme.”

My head popped up, and the only thing on my mind was murder. I knew the fuck they didn’t take one of mine! Charlotte wasn’t ready for what I was capable of.

Chapter 8

"Play the opening like a book, the middle game like a magician, and the endgame like a machine."

Ki'Asia

The entire plane ride, my thoughts were clouded with Preme. Preme was the only thing my father and aunt Chan had left of their brother, Allen. Although we weren't as close as Pop and I were, we were still family, and there was nothing he wouldn't do for me if I was in need and vice versa.

After Trapp informed us of the news that day, we went straight over to his house. They killed my cousin walking into his home; shot him a total of nineteen times. From what we gathered, somebody had to have followed him. I wasn't even understanding who, because we were too careful for that and had eyes everywhere. That's why I knew when my house was shot up, it had to be either someone from my team, or someone had followed Tyleek, which we were leaning toward the latter.

"You good, ma?" Tyleek looked down at me and asked. I looked up into his eyes and nodded my head. Had it not been for him, Desiree, Trapp, and my mom—surprisingly—these last two days would have been pure hell. Even Da'Jon didn't know what to say or do. He was hurting just as bad as I was.

The flight attendant made the landing announcement, and Tyleek and I fastened our seat belts. Even though this was not going to be a memorable occasion the entire time, considering Preme's body was shipped back to NY and the funeral would be held here, I was still excited about seeing my father and aunt.

Once we landed, Tyleek grabbed our bags from the overhead, and we made our way to the baggage area to get the rest of our stuff. When we made it outside, I was praying I didn't have to try to catch a cab, and I damn sure wasn't about to try to jump on no train, bus, or anything else from LaGuardia, but lo and behold, I heard someone yelling my name. *Prayers answered!*

"Poooooot! Ki'Asiaaaaaa!" I turned to my left and saw my aunt and ran full speed ahead into her arms.

When I pulled back from her and looked at her face, I could see the stress in her eyes. It was taking a toll on her to have to be the one to bury Preme. With my father locked up and Preme's mother somewhere strung out, Preme was my aunt Chan's responsibility, so I knew it was killing her.

For a brief—and just a brief—moment, I forgot Tyleek was there.

"Oh, Aunty. This is my boo, Tyleek," I said, introducing the two.

Tyleek went to shake her hand, but she grabbed him in a hug instead.

"Boy, you family. We don't do that here," she told him after she released him. "Grab y'all bags and let's go. I'm double parked and am not getting a ticket behind y'all asses," she said, laughing, walking off.

My aunt was doing the damn thing. She had a pearl white 2011 Nissan Armada Platinum, sitting on some twenty-two's like her ass was still in her twenties.

Once we got settled in the truck, I started on the clowning.

"Aunty, what you know about twenty-two's?" I asked,

and Tyleek and I both burst out laughing.

"Girl, ya big-head ass cousin put that shit on my truck. Shit look ugly as fuck."

"How is Mack doing? He don't wanna relocate to the Queen City with his little cousin?" I questioned about her oldest son.

"Poot, Mack ass ain't going nowhere. That dude eat and shit Brooklyn. He said that's all he knows, and that's all he wants to know," she told me, and I simply nodded my head.

As we drove, she and Tyleek conversed, and I tuned them out, taking in the sights. I remembered NY clear as day, despite the fact that I was young when we moved to Charlotte. It felt good at times to be back home around the hustle and bustle of the city. We were about ten minutes out from Brooklyn when my aunt made mention of the funeral.

"So it's not going to be this long, drawn-out ceremony. I want to put my nephew in the ground and be over with it, feel me? I already feel like I failed his father, and I just can't deal with having a big funeral. It's going to be extended to family and close friends, and that's it."

"I understand, Aunty. And trust, we will get to the bottom of it," I told her.

She looked over at me when we got to the stoplight. "I know you will. You better."

Both Tyleek and I nodded our heads in agreement. Once we pulled up on the block, I could not believe anything looked any different than it had the last time I'd been here last summer. I usually went to see my father often, but since he was in PA, I didn't come up to NY just to go. That was ass backwards. I did it this time because I'd missed her, and considering what happened with Preme, I didn't want her to have to face it without me. Yeah, I felt somewhat at fault for that. If it weren't for protecting me, half of the crew from NY that was in Charlotte wouldn't even be there. So just like she felt she'd failed him, I felt some of the weight of that as well.

"Well look at little Poot!" I heard Mack yell as soon as my feet touched the ground. My aunt had a nice little crib on Bergen between Saratoga and Thomas Boyland, which I'd forever call Hopkinson. For the life of me, I could never understand the name change.

"And yo' ass ain't been to see your little cousin yet!" I replied, getting squished in the bear hug he had me in.

Nodding his head, "And who dis?" he asked, directing his attention at Tyleek.

"First, can we get inside before all the pleasantries? But don't act like you getting ready to try to strong arm my man or nothing, 'cause I'll square up wit' yo' big ass!" I said to Mack, causing all them to start laughing.

"Firm, man," Tyleek said, dapping Mack up.

"Damn, at least you got some manners, son. This one here just wanna fight all the damn time." He shook his head as he grabbed the one bag I had placed down, and we headed up the stairs to the first floor of my aunt's house.

I used to love coming over here when we were younger, considering we stayed in the hood. Regardless of how much money my father made, leaving Garvey was never an option for him. My aunt's house had three bedrooms and a bathroom on each floor, and a fully furnished basement which she gave to Mack when he turned eighteen, seeing as how she knew she'd never be able to get rid of him.

After we got settled in, we headed to the first floor where my aunt was taking food out the oven. Off tis, I knew that it was curry chicken, and she knew that was my favorite dish from her. I helped her set the table while Mack took Tyleek outside to meet some of the crew up here—some in which I hadn't seen in forever myself.

When they came back in, Mack and Tyleek had Biggz and Pop with them, who had flown up Monday. Biggz reached out and hugged me first and then Pop, and they both repeated it with my aunt Chan. Initially, I was still somewhat leery of them both, but after what happened with Preme, I knew that if it was someone on my team, it wasn't those two. Pop was ready to set the city of Charlotte on fire, and Biggz was right behind him. Tyleek, on the other hand, wasn't too convinced.

He dealt mostly with my guys now since he'd taken over as the face of Murda, and he said it was always some controversy over who was assigned what and why they weren't in the loop of certain things. In the past couple weeks alone, he said they'd been in at least two arguments.

I tried to get him to understand that they were family and family did that, even when they were up under my reign, but he wasn't letting it go.

After my aunt got all the food on the table, Mack led us in grace and we dug in. It was quiet as a mouse with the exception of some smacking and forks and spoons hitting the plate. That's how serious it was. Chan's ass threw down in the kitchen, and when she cooked, we never came to play.

"So Tyleek, how long have you and my niece been seeing each other since my first time hearing about you was when she asked me to get you put on Divine's visitation list?" my aunt Chan asked.

Pop cleared his throat and smirked, and I shot his ass the middle finger.

"Actually, Ki'Asia and I dated for a while when we were in high school. I was two years ahead of her, and she thought I was just this ho out here in the streets, and she broke my little heart," Tyleek replied, hand over heart, feigning hurt. Although I was blushing, I wanted to take his head straight off his shoulders.

"That's not the complete truth. I just don't like unfriendly competition, and back then, I didn't believe in chasing anything other than them books and a dollar. He wasn't getting ready to add me to his stable," I clarified, causing my aunt to laugh.

"That's cute. Y'all was on y'all little high school shit, and now years later, y'all on that king and queen shit. I'm wit' it."

Mack needed to stay his ass from around my aunt talking slang, because I swear it sounded like I was talking to a twenty-something-year-old as opposed to my father's oldest sibling. She was a queen her damn self, and when need be, her guns barked louder than anyone's, with her short, sneaky ass.

"Some things are just meant to be," Tyleek said, causing me to blush even harder.

We made small talk, laughing and joking while feasting on the bomb triple-layer chocolate cake my aunt had made for dessert. Listening to everybody laugh made me feel good, despite the loss we'd taken.

Around an hour later, Pop and Biggz headed out, and

Mack headed out to hit the block. He asked Tyleek if he wanted to go out with him, but of course, he declined, talking about he wanted to make sure I was good. Little did he know, after all that food, the only thing on my mind was curling up in bed and knocking out.

After we both helped out with helping my aunt clean the kitchen, we went upstairs, showered, and headed to bed. My head wasn't on the pillow for five seconds before I started getting an unsettling feeling in my stomach.

I darted up from the bed and ran to the bathroom, regurgitating everything that I'd eaten earlier. Tyleek was right behind me.

"I would pick now to get sick. Probably because I haven't had no curry in a while," I said and shrugged my shoulders.

"Or probably because you been having all this unprotected dick up in yo' ass. It ain't like you on birth control, ma," Tyleek said, and he was a thousand percent right. We'd been having sex any time we were alone in each other's presence, and birth control had been the farthest thing from my mind. However, I wasn't willing to accept that just yet.

“Nah, that can’t be it. I’m telling you, it’s probably what I ate, babe.”

His hand stayed planted on my back, and he smirked at me as he walked me back to the room. As soon as my head hit the pillow, I was out like a light.

Saturday morning...

We were in the car by five thirty to head to Lewisburg, the prison my father was in. I kept stealing glances at Tyleek, and he seemed to be nervous, so I decided to fuck with him a little bit.

“Babe, what’s wrong? You worried that you might not be good enough for Divine’s princess?”

“Poot, you dead ass wrong. Leave that man alone,” my aunt said, and we burst out laughing. Tyleek sat in the back seat looking at me like he wanted to kill me in that instant. I knew he was apprehensive when it came to meeting my pops, but he really had nothing to worry about.

One thing about Divine, if he was nothing else, he was

fair. As long as the man I was with treated me good, had a head on his shoulders, and didn't have me looking like a fool in the streets, he was good. And a dude putting their hands on me was a death sentence, but my pops didn't have to worry about that. I'd be the executioner in that situation.

"I'm good. You know, Divine is just somewhat of a legend in the game. It's actually gonna be an honor to meet the man." To hear Tyleek say those things about my father made me feel proud. Not saying I was proud of the things my father had done, but I understood his reasoning wholeheartedly.

There was no room for feelings in this game. Taking lives came with a part of it. If you were in this game and put your faith and trust in the next man without knowing there was no loyalty in this, you'd be the one dead as opposed to burying your enemy. Every move you made had to be strategically thought out, which was another reason I was thankful for this visit because we needed his help.

I fell asleep on the short two-and-a-half-hour ride and woke up feeling like shit. My stomach was cutting cartwheels, and my mouth was wetter than normal.

"Poot, what's wrong?" my aunt questioned when we stepped out of the truck.

"Nothing, Aunty. I'm—" My sentence was cut short by me leaning over and puking all over the ground. "—pregnant," I finished the sentence.

Both her eyes and Tyleek's eyes grew wide before a grin spread across his face. He went to walk toward me, and I looked at him with a look that told him he'd better practice the two-feet rule. He smirked as my aunt hugged me, telling me how excited she was and how my father was going to stroke out. All I wanted to do was get back in the car and go back to sleep.

My aunt went to the back of her truck and grabbed a pack of facial wipes and a bottle of Crest mouthwash out of a tote bag. I looked up at her when she came back over to me with it, with a confused look on my face.

"Aunty, you keep stuff like this in your trunk?"

"Heifer, I ain't got no man. That's my travel bag when I go see them niggas," she told me, and my stomach was feeling too queasy for me to laugh, so I just shook my head.

"You a mess," I told her.

When we walked in, we were asked for our identification and searched before being sent to an area where my father would be joining us. My aunt told me he had some surprise for me, but I couldn't imagine what it could be. To pass time before they started bringing the prisoners out, we made idle talk about nothing. Now that I'd allowed reality to set in and accepted the fact that I could possibly be pregnant, I was nervous as hell, especially to say anything to my dad. I was so into my thoughts that his voice scared the shit outta me.

"Dang, baby girl. You can't even get up and greet ya old man?"

My head whipped around so fast, and I had to remember they had rules about the affection shown, but I jumped on my daddy like I was still the same five-year-old that loved to see her daddy come through the door. Most of the guards and I got along anyway, and they knew it had been a while since I'd been up here. Either way, nothing was going to stop me from showing my daddy some love.

He released me, and that handsome smile and those

deep dimples appeared, and my ass got all emotional. My dad was already buff, but he had gotten even more buffed since the last time I'd seen him. If I must say so myself, my daddy was fine.

"Look at you, baby girl. You so damn pretty, looking like me," he said, arm around my shoulder, grinning brightly. My daddy was almost a foot taller than me, so he had to look down at me. It was the cutest thing in the world when we were together.

Before sitting down, my father gave Chan a hug, and I introduced him to Tyleek. As my aunt did when she first met him, Tyleek went to reach his hand out to shake my father's, but my father gave him a hug like he'd known him for years.

"Tyleek, aka Mr. Firm. I've heard a lot about you," my father said to Tyleek, and he looked shocked.

My father started laughing. "All good things, son. Don't even worry about it."

I could see the tension release from Tyleek's face, and I let out a little chuckle.

"So aside from being almost hitched, what's been

going on wit' you, baby girl? And congrats on the club," my daddy said, and I put my head down, smiling.

"I've just been maintaining. I've decided to stay on as a paralegal for a while longer, keeping up with the funeral home, butcher shop, and the other two clubs. Soooo, I stay pretty busy," I told him.

"Good, good. And how is Da'Jon?"

"He's OK. He came to the grand opening. He was going to come up for the funeral, but he'd already taken time off for the opening, and he didn't want to miss any more school time. You know he think he's got a baby on the way." *Ah damn. Why in the hell did I bring up baby?*

"Ah shit, now. I'm too young to be a granddaddy. I'll holler at his knuckle head ass about that. And what's up wit' ya momma? How her and Mr. Walt doing?"

"Well, you know mom and I don't see eye to eye too much, but lately, she's been cool. They're good. Ohhhh, they got married a while back. I was supposed to have a reception for them at Essence, but Walt was on the road, so Mom had to cancel it at the last minute." I noticed he was smiling but looking behind me.

"Speaking of marriage, I have someone I want you to meet, baby girl."

I turned in the direction my father was looking and saw a pretty chocolate Amazon of a female. I mean, she was simply gorgeous. She wore her hair in a natural up-do and was dressed very conservatively. Even under the loose outfit she wore, you could tell she had curves for days. I wouldn't say my face bore a scrunched-up look but probably more of confusion since I saw that my father was absolutely enthralled with her appearance.

When he stood to greet her, he gave her a lingering hug and kiss, and I knew right then that this had to be the woman he mentioned that was holding him down.

"Ki'Asia, Tyleek... I'd like y'all to meet my queen, Asaada. Queen, this is my baby girl, Ki'Asia, and her king and also soon to be child's father, Tyleek," my daddy said and looked over at me.

My eyes shot open wide, and Tyleek's mouth dropped—I saw it from my peripheral. My aunt Chan thought it was the funniest shit in the world, and Asaada wore a huge smile on her face.

Both Tyleek and I stood to hug her, and when I sat back down, I had to ask the million-dollar question.

"Daddy... how did you know? I mean, I still haven't confirmed it yet. I-I-I was going to say something, but, I mean... how did you know?"

You would have thought my aunt was watching *Kings of Comedy* or some shit with how hard she was laughing.

"You have a glow about you, Queen. I noticed it as soon as I looked in your eyes," Asaada answered instead of my father.

I didn't know whether to hide, run, or just pass the hell out. I just knew for sure my father was getting ready to have a conniption.

"And you thicker than a Snicker. I'm not upset, princess, before you go thinking I am. Look at you. You have three clubs, a funeral home, a butcher shop, and you're a paralegal. On top of that, you make sure you hold your old man down. You're doing everything you're supposed to do as woman, and—no shade, Firm—don't need a man for shit. And you're doing it all at the age of twenty-two. I'm damn proud of you," he told me, and tears welled up in my eyes.

"Thank you, Daddy. That means a lot," I replied, as I reached across the table and placed my hand on top of his free hand.

"But look, y'all ladies get to know each other a little bit. Let me slide over here and holler at Firm for a minute," he said, and his face became blank. Tyleek must have noticed the change because, once again, he looked like he was about to pass out.

By no means was Tyleek a punk, and he proved that a million times over, but my father's demeanor had a way of doing that to even the strongest person. He could be cold or hot, and whichever he was, you never knew what was on his mind. He could kill with a smile and walk away from it as if nothing had happened.

My dad signaled to someone with a nod of the head, and the man gave a short nod in return which prompted my father to tell Firm to follow him, and they walked over to a table on the other side of the room. Shoot, I was nervous for Tyleek my damn self, but I zoomed in on the conversation with the ladies. Inside, I was praying for the best outcome with those two.

Firm

I was nervous about Ki'Asia's father calling me over, thinking his reason was to tell me he didn't think I was it for his daughter. I mean, I didn't get that with how he acted toward me, but you could never be too sure.

"Aight, Firm, so it's like this. I've been hearing some great things about you and the way you've been handling business in Charlotte. Now, my only concern is this little situation that needs to be handled immediately, feel me?"

His brow raised, and I knew what he was talking about, so I nodded my head and leaned in a little closer to hear what he had to say.

"I don't know if you know much about why I'm up in here, but let me give you a little rundown.

When I relocated my prince and princess, along with their mother, to Charlotte, it was to expand my dealings in the game and a few other things. It was taking a little longer than I expected, but I finally got it done. Well, niggas up here thought they could sleep on ole Divine since I was OT, and decided they were going to attempt a takeover on my spots. When I got word of the shit, I was livid.

I made the conscious decision to head back to NY and hold courts in the streets. I was the judge, jury, and executioner. One man, one plan, multiple hands. And what I mean by that is I was the mastermind behind the plan, but I made sure that not only my hands were involved. It was impossible for only mine to be anyway.

It's always good to have people in high places on your team, and I'm talking about more than just greasing a few palms at the police station. See, what princess did when she got involved with law—that shit was brilliant. But she still doesn't even utilize the resources that she has at her fingertips. That's where you come in."

For almost an hour, the street legend himself schooled me on what I needed to do to get at Dreek's team, and I must admit the shit was brilliant. The only thing I knew was going to be an issue was the fact that he wanted Ki'Asia to step all the way back from the street shit until this blew over. Now, that was like telling a damn pit bull not to attack when it knew its owner was in danger, so I didn't know how that part of it was going to fly. But at the same time, considering she could very well be pregnant, while carrying my seed, she didn't have much of a choice.

After we wrapped up our conversation and he mentally programmed my number, we headed back over to the table with the ladies. Ki'Asia's aunt went to the vending machines to get snacks for everyone while we talked and laughed. I enjoyed seeing a completely softer side to Ki'Asia. She was like mush around her father and became this innocent little girl, and the shit was cute.

At the end of the visit, her hormones must have been in overdrive, because she cried like she was never going to see Divine again. He whispered something in her ear that caused the tears to dry up and a wide smile to spread across her face. Knowing her and after meeting him, there was no telling what he said to make her smile like that. Hell, he could have told her she needed to go kill her first-grade teacher, and she would have had that same smile.

Everyone else said their goodbyes to Divine, Ki'Asia got Asaada's phone number, and we headed out to take the trip back to NY.

During the ride, Ki'Asia's ass passed out again, and

Chan was in another world as she drove, so it allowed me time with my thoughts. If everything went according to the plan Divine set up for me to execute, we could have Dreek's whole team eliminated in a matter of days and not have to worry about any more casualties on our end.

I texted my uncle Jackson to have him do some digging for me and told him I needed the info like yesterday. I then hit up Trapp and told him I needed everyone, including foot soldiers, to meet at the warehouse Thursday at 9 p.m. It was time to bring this shit to an end once and for all.

***

"OK, Aunty. I promise it won't be this long again," Ki'Asia told her as we got ready to head into the airport. Preme's funeral was yesterday, and Ki'Asia couldn't attend because she was sick. Although I knew she wanted to say her final goodbyes, I was kind of glad she was under the weather. I didn't do funerals like that unless it was someone close, but to see those closest to her break down the way they did would have killed her, and I knew it because it broke me.

Her aunt had been holding up while we were here, but

she took it the hardest. Chan and Ki'Asia were extremely close—more like mother and daughter as opposed to aunt and niece—so I knew it would have killed her to see her aunt literally try to join Preme in the casket.

After I gave Chan a hug, we made our way through check-in and security and were headed back to Charlotte. No soon as we got on the plane and I put our tote bags in the overhead, Ki'Asia was out like a light. Plane hadn't even taken off and she was already snoring.

I was getting ready to take her lead, when a text message came through on my phone. When I looked down, I wished I had turned the shit off. This dumb bitch, Tricie, was sending me a picture of a sonogram. I immediately hit her back and told her I'd hit her up a little later and turned my phone off. I laid back in the seat and sighed. I didn't know what Tricie was trying to prove, but for her sake, she'd better hope I got my mind right before I met up with her.

That nap I tried to take never came with all the thoughts that were consuming my mind. It was a very strong possibility that Ki could be pregnant, and at this point, I didn't want anything stressing her out. Then this situation with taking out Dreek's team, which was probably the easiest out of all my problems after speaking with Divine. Tricie's issue wasn't my issue, but since she wanted to make it my issue, I was going to handle it for her.

Once the flight attendant announced that we were fifteen minutes from landing, I gently nudged Ki'Asia to wake her up. When I looked over at her, it was like I fell in love all over again. I didn't just want her to be a baby momma.

I wanted her to be my wife. I looked down at her stomach and didn't see how anyone could have missed it before. I knew she was getting thicker, but I never paid attention to her stomach area since her being pregnant didn't cross my mind until she got sick. She had a little pudge that was noticeable and wasn't there before. *My ass is about to be a father*, I thought to myself. Yeah, this shit had to come to an end with Dreek and Tricie both before my prince or princess came into this world.

"Babe, we there?" Ki'Asia asked, eyes still closed.

"We landing shortly, ma. Get up."

She opened her eyes and turned in my direction. "When we get home, are you going to tell me what you and my father talked about?" she asked.

I knew this was coming sooner or later, but I was hoping I'd have time to think of something before then. It was no way in hell I wanted to feel this girl's wrath behind me telling her to fall all the way back, but it was what needed to be done.

"Yeah, baby, I got you."

"Oh... and you can tell me who that was that texted you and put you in a funk right before we took off." She had her lips pulled up in a little pout, but she'd shocked the shit outta me with that one.

"Mm hmm. I heard you sighing, nigga." I kissed her forehead and let out a chuckle before we tightened our seat belts and prepared for landing.

Trapp was waiting outside at the airport, so we loaded our bags and had us to drop us off at Ki'Asia's crib. On the ride over, we talked about a little bit of shit that had been going on with the team, but not wanting to say too much in front of Ki'Asia, I kept the conversation short.

"So what's been up with you and Desiree? Y'all still an item, or was it just a one-night thing?" Ki'Asia asked, laughing.

"Nah, ain't no one night thing. Shorty straight. She just got an attitude from hell on her. She slapped the shit out of one of your dancers Friday night for telling her she wasn't coming in the following night. Damn girl just ruthless. I like that feisty shit, though. Tame her little ass right on down," his clown ass said, causing Ki'Asia to damn near cry from laughing so hard.

"Well, we got something to tell y'all, but we'll plan something special to inform everyone all at once. For now, just hurry the hell up and get me home if you want that new car smell to still be in your car," she told him.

He shot me a look, and I just shrugged my shoulders. I wasn't going to mention it to anyone until it was confirmed and she was ready. Until then, I wasn't opening my mouth.

Trapp helped me take the bags we had in the house, we dapped up, and then he dipped. When I turned to lock the door and set the alarm, Ki'Asia had already gone upstairs. Grabbing my phone from my pocket, I turned it back on and before it was on completely, it was vibrating out of control. I knew it wasn't anything urgent because we'd just left Trapp, and he didn't say anything alarming. I looked down at the phone once the screen brightened and started seeing a number that wasn't saved in addition to Tricie's. *What the fuck is going on?*

As I walked up the steps, I began reading a few texts, and all of them were from a female I'd dealt with some years back, right after I got out of school. She was saying it was urgent that she talk to me, could I please get in touch with her, it's very important, yadda, yadda. Now *that* was the last thing on my mind. Hell, right now, I didn't even want to deal with Tricie's ass.

I heard the shower going when I entered the room and immediately began stepping out of my clothes. I was gon' fuck Ki'Asia into a coma and pray she didn't want to talk about Divine or anything else. All I wanted was a shower, some sleep, and some pussy—out of order.

When I stepped in the shower, she had her head up

under the showerhead, letting the water beat down over her body. Ki'Asia was a damn sight for sore eyes. Her body was just perfect, and she was all mine. My hands began roaming the places my eyes had just left, and once I got to that treasure box between her legs, I slowly started fiddling her clit. She must have been just as horny as I was because she turned around and damn near attacked my ass. I had to make sure I was good and stuck against the shower wall in order not to fall.

Baby girl dropped to her knees and took my entire length into that warm, wet mouth of hers, causing my toes to make love to each other. I mean, they were all on top of each other. As my dick slid in and out of her mouth, she began massaging my sac. Once she removed her hands, I knew I was in trouble as her mouth alternated back and forth between the two, sucking and gobbling! Baby girl literally put it all in her mouth and hummed on it.

I went to pull her hair head back by her hair so she could know I was getting ready to cum, but she slapped my hand out the way and locked my shit in a death grip. I couldn't pull from her mouth if I tried.

"Gottttt damn, girl!" I yelled out as she swallowed my soldiers. And she didn't get up until my dick was damn near dry again.

"Turn that ass over!" I grabbed her by the arm and spun her around, making her place her hands on the shower wall in front of her.

I didn't know what had come over me, but I lifted her by the waist from behind and showed no mercy as I stuck every inch in her.

"Firmmmmm! Oh my Goooooodddddd! Baby... please... slow... down! Aggghhhh!" she screamed out, but I had blocked her out. It was wrong for me to do it, but I remembered the text message I got from Denice, the girl I'd dealt with right out of high school, and I was remembering when I walked in on her getting ate the fuck out in my bed that I paid for, screaming out another nigga's name. He was my first kill, and the only thing that saved that ho's life was the fact she told me she was pregnant.

After that, I'd never heard from her again, and

honestly, I didn't care to. Fuck that bitch and everything she stood for!

Ki'Asia's screams were damn near terrifying, and that's what brought me back to reality. Well... that and the fact I had shot my load off. When I let her down, she turned around and smacked the shit outta my ass.

"Nigga, what the fuck is wrong wit' you! I'm screaming for yo' ass to stop, and the more I scream, the harder you fuckin' go! I should shoot yo' ass!" she yelled as she opened the shower door and stormed off into the bedroom.

Fuck! Denice texting my ass threw me off my shit, and although I said I didn't give a damn what she wanted, I knew I needed to reach out to her. Wasn't no feelings there or nothing like that, but when I fucked with her, she was kind of like a lookout for me, and if she said it was urgent that she needed to speak to me, I could only wonder what it was about... especially since her father was the damn district attorney.

After grabbing a towel, I walked into the bedroom, and Ki'Asia was laying on her side with tears flowing down her face. I felt fucked up like hell. There was no way I meant to hurt my girl, and damn sure not over thinking about the next chick. I lay behind her and pulled her close to me, and I could hear her light sniffles.

"My bad, ma. I zoned out. I'm sorry, baby. You know that ain't even like me."

"Whatever, Firm. I'm good on you," she said, and I knew she was mad as hell. Ki'Asia only called me Firm during business, sex, and when she was mad.

I kissed her shoulders gently while rubbing her stomach, which made her relax a little bit.

"So now you gon' tell me what you and my daddy talked about?" she questioned. Since I'd fucked up, I'd rather tell her and have her talk to me than to have her mad at me.

"Yeah." I released her and rolled over on my back, then ran my hand down my face, dreading this conversation.

When she rolled over and faced me, arm propped up and head on her hand, I knew there was no escaping it.

"I'ma take over, and I need you to stand down. You

won't have shit to do with the day-to-day aspects of the business. You won't know anything. The only thing you'll do is run the legal business until we know for a fact this shit with Dreek's team is taken care of. And trust, it will be taken care of.

I was met with pure silence, making me damn near afraid to look over at her. I didn't intimidate easily, but Ki'Asia's ass was a different kind of crazy. Like... I used to say she was the female version of me, but hell no. If you got on her bad side, the level of crazy she went to didn't exist. There was no name for it.

"And plus, you need to be worried about the baby," I added in there to soften her up some before I looked at her. See... this the shit I was talking about. Her ass was sitting up here looking in my face wearing a big ass grin.

"The fuck, Ki!"

"OK!" She kissed me on the lips and then rolled over. Five minutes later, she was snoring lightly. Bet you my ass wasn't about to be snoring lightly anytime soon. I was keeping one eye open around little cuckoo!

Chapter 9

"It is always better to sacrifice your opponent's men."

Ki'Asia

If Firm and my father thought I was going to sit back and not do a damn thing to take down the muthafuckas that were trying to destroy an empire that *I* got to where it needed to be, they really had lost their minds. This was my shit, and there was no way in hell I was just sitting back and not doing anything.

For every move Firm made for a two-month period, I had one up on his ass. He had my supervisor looking into key members on Dreek's team—their criminal records, addresses, everything. The only thing I didn't know was when he planned to do this attack. My father should have known better than to try and pull one over on me.

See, I knew when Firm said that he was going to handle everything and for me to fall back, my father was getting ready to send in reinforcement and go in for the entire kill.

There would be nothing tied to Dreek. Not even a child. My father was a firm believer that you could breed a child to take over in your footsteps, and he wasn't leaving any room for error, so he was eliminating everything... simultaneously.

Once I found the information Jackson had dug up, in addition to me going behind Tyleek's back and speaking to Officer Black, whom he thought I didn't know, I had not only all the information on every key player but side players as well, including Dreek's connect which was a local. And when I said local, I didn't mean Charlotte or surrounding areas. Nigga just wasn't on a scale to be making noise out of country with the weak ass product his team was pushing. My only issue with getting involved in this entire thing, was the pregnancy.

The week after we got back from NY, that Monday, it was confirmed with my doctor that I was indeed pregnant, and further along than I thought. Evidently, it was possible to still have some bleeding while you were pregnant, and since I had only missed my cycle for two months, I'd assumed I was only two months. Imagine my and Tyleek's surprise when the doctor said we were four months along with a little princess, who had her legs gapped wide open on the sonogram. So now I was six months, big as hell, and miserable. Yes, a fat, miserable fuck!

"Girl, you need to sit yo' ass down somewhere talking 'bout you gon' kill that girl. If she's pregnant, it was before your time, so what difference does it make?"

Desiree sat here trying to convince me not to make this child suffer. What everyone failed to realize, I saw the damn sonogram Tyleek tried to hide from me in his phone. When I questioned him, he said he wasn't worried about the baby and he wasn't going to keep talking about the shit. In addition to the sonogram, I also saw he was meeting up with some damn bitch about something that they weren't discussing through text, and I was going to get to the bottom of that as well. Did I think he was cheating? Hell no. He knew I'd cut his balls off and serve them up for Thanksgiving dinner, but was he being a sneaky ass? Yes, he was, and my emotional self did not have time for it.

"I'm just going to talk to the damn girl, and you shut up and don't tell nobody where I'm going. If he calls or comes by, you just tell him that you don't know where I'm at."

Before she could say anything else, I grabbed my purse and waddled out of the office with her yelling, "Firm gon' spank dat ass!"

I got in my car and headed over to Tricie's house, determined for once and for all to get to the bottom of this baby situation. Tyleek wasn't aware that I'd done a little background search on Ms. Tricie Brooks after I ran into her at the club, but he'd find out. Letting him 'handle it' was taking too long, and I needed to have some fun.

I was dressed as a social worker, just in case anyone saw me, or things got kind of ugly, and I had on a curly wig with light brown highlights. When I pulled up in front of her house, I reached in my glove compartment and grabbed my little Family Dollar reading glasses and threw them on then reached in the back seat and grabbed my briefcase. Of course, one of my burners was in my briefcase, along with some torture tools in case I felt adventurous. Like the AMEX commercial said... never left home without 'em.

Ding, dong... ding, dong... ding, dong, ding, dong!

I chuckled inwardly as her bell recited the theme from the granddaddy clock in my living room. *Bourgeois ass!*

"Who is it?" I heard from behind the door and knew it was Tricie.

"Ms. Martin with Mecklenburg County Department of Social Services. I'd just like a moment of your time, umm... Ms. Tricie Brooks." Acting like I didn't know her name, I glanced down at the clipboard in case she was looking through the peephole and put on the most proper accent I could muster up.

Once she opened the door, I looked at her, and she was huge. She looked like she was going to pop at any moment. I saw she hadn't taken heed to my warning which upset me a great deal. Tsk, tsk. Some people never learned.

"Hello, come in," she said all chipper, not knowing I was two seconds away from killing her ass. I didn't give a damn if she was pregnant or not. I distinctly gave her an order, and she didn't follow through with it. Oh, she thought this shit was a joke? Well it wasn't!

"You can follow me to the living room. I see you have

a little one on the way yourself," she said, and I looked up at her with a fake smile plastered on my face.

"Yes, I sure do. And great. This won't take long at all. Um... if you don't mind, can I get a cup of water please?"

"Oh yes, sure. Would you like some ice? Lemon? Splenda?"

She couldn't be serious right now. I knew good and damn well she couldn't be serious.

"Just some ice, please. Thank you so much!"

I needed to hurry up and do what I had to do then get the hell up outta here. This chick was completely freaking bonkers.

As she went to the kitchen to get the water, I popped opened my briefcase and pulled out the short rubber gloves, ultrasound gel, stethoscope, a scalpel, and a pair of trauma shears. I placed the items on the side of table and yelled out, "Can you bring a cup of hot water as well!"

"Um... OK!" she yelled back.

I was so excited. My baby started moving around and it was as if she knew her mother was in her zone. I started to clap, but that would have been a little too extra.

Grabbing my trusted .380 from the briefcase, I put it in the band of my waist just as I heard her making her way back to the living room.

"OK, here you go. One glass of water and... What is all of that?" she asked once she made it in the living room, wearing a look of confusion on her face. I removed the gun from behind my back and signaled for her to have a seat. She wasn't moving. I removed the wig from my head and the glasses from over my eyes, which caused her to drop the cup with the hot water as she recognized who I was.

"Damn, damn, damn! I needed that, Tricie. Sit yo' scared ass down!" I lectured her. I really needed that cup of water. I wanted all the tools to be as sterile as possible.

"Please, please, please don't hurt me, Ki'Asia. I promise, I'll leave town, I'll do whatever you want me to do. Just please don't hurt me. I'll leave Tyleek alone. Just... just... just please don't hurt me," she said then started sobbing.

I stood there unbothered in the least. "Lay down on your back, Tricie. Didn't I tell you that I was going to rip that baby out of you and rearrange your uterus? Did you think I was playing? Huh?" I smiled as I placed the gun on the table and grabbed the ultrasound gel and stethoscope.

"Umm... umm... Oh my God. Umm... I'm not pregnant," she said and started crying louder. The look on my face couldn't be described. My head was pulled back a little, and I know I was confused—just had to be. I started walking closer to her.

"What you mean you're not pregnant? It doesn't take a rocket scientist to see that—aarrgghhhhhhh, you stupid bitch!" I yelled as I went to lift her shirt and saw she had a silicone belly strapped around her. I had to touch it to see what the hell it felt like. "Oh my damn! What in the hell is wrong with you! You made me bring my good shit over here, thinking I'm about to deliver a damn baby, and you walking around with a... ohhhhh, you's a sick bitch, you know that?"

I was disgusted with this ho. Then it dawned on me that she sent Tyleek a sonogram picture. "But what about the sonogram picture? Where the hell did you get the sonogram picture?"

She sat there crying like she'd lost her damn dog or

something, but she was getting ready to answer some damn questions. Oh, she could best believe she was getting ready to answer some damn questions!

"Little girl... if you don't answer my damn question, fake pregnant ass and all, I will still make good on my promise and rip your uterus out. But unlike my initial plans to be gentle, I will *fuck* your intestines up! Now answer me, damn it!" I yelled. I was trembling because I was so damn confused and hurt. I think I was more hurt because I really wanted to have some fun by torturing a muthafucka today, and that wasn't going to happen.

"My... my friend... my friend is pregnant, and she's using my name and insurance information. The sonogram was hers," she stated, and my eyes bulged out their sockets damn near.

"So wait... you did all this for what? To get Firm back?"

"I knew that if I was carrying his child, he'd come back to me. She was going to give me the baby, but you've ruined it now! You just had to ruin—"

"Bitch, shut the fuck up. I mean, I don't even know

how the hell Tyleek dealt wit' yo' ass for so long. You got the body of a black girl, but yo' ass dumb as rocks, and your voice? Oh my God, you sound like a bourgeois ass white girl! Not even ya average white girls. The kind society make 'em out to be. You just fucking disgust me. Like he wasn't gon' get a DNA test. Just so stupid! And they say I'm crazy. I cannot believe this shit!

Let me leave you with this to take in the afterlife. Maybe you'll meet one of the twelve disciples or somebody, Moses, Peter, John, some damn body, and remember Ki'Asia Synese Barron told you this. Having a baby don't keep a man that don't wanna be kept, mm kay? You never had that man's heart. Hell, you never even had a title. A baby was going to be an eighteen-year plus sentence for you to have to see him with the next woman, raising your child, with other children that he actually wanted." I shook my head before I reached in the briefcase and grabbed a belt along with the hotshots and a pen and pad.

"What you're getting ready to do is write a letter to your dearest Tyleek explaining to him just how pathetic you really are. Here," I told her, giving her the pen and paper, and picked the gun up and held it to her head just for some motivation.

As she wrote the letter, I sat there thanking my lucky stars that I was never this pressed over a man and would never be. I didn't see how females really felt that a baby was the answer to their problems when their spot wasn't even secured with the man. Once she finished, I placed the letter and gun on the table.

"Now this won't hurt at all," I told her as I sat on her ass, tied the belt around her arm, and injected her with two hotshots for good measure. She went from leaning to convulsing to meeting her maker.

After packing up the briefcase, I went in the kitchen and looked for a broom to clean up the mess she'd made when she dropped the glass. Once everything was cleaned up, I went to the bathroom to secure the wig back on my head, put on the glasses. I knew I was slipping mentally, going into a dark space, and I needed to get back to reality fast. I shook it off and headed out the front door. When I got in the car, I shot a text to my homey Doug at Brinks

Security and told him to remove all traces from the video footage of me being there.

I drove to the club in a daze. I was still baffled at the lengths this girl was willing to go to get Tyleek back in her good graces. Tyleek was a good man, true indeed, but he was never her man. He had some bomb sex, yes Lord, I'd shout that from the rooftops, but that was ultimately all they shared. Her life ended for some dick on a whim. And I could have let her live and just wallow in her own misery, but some people were just too bat shit crazy to walk the earth. Before any of you say shit, I wasn't one of them. I had my reasons for being the way I was. Her? Dick and money ruled her world, and people like that just didn't deserve to live because they ultimately had nothing to live for.

The wig and glasses were snatched off on the drive over to the club, so when I pulled up, I just grabbed my purse, made sure my gun was secured, and headed inside the club. I spoke to a few of the girls who were getting ready to set up for their shift on the third floor, and I thought I had a card game going on tonight as well, because I saw a few dudes coming in that looked like they were heavy spenders.

One dude in particular caught my eye, and I had to look around and make sure I wasn't being punked. There was no way in hell he'd walked up in here. He must have noticed me the same time I'd noticed him. Our eyes met, and a smirk appeared on his cocky ass face. That was my cue to keep it pushing to my office. But before I could get far, Desiree stopped me at the bar.

"I know got damn well you wasn't getting ready to walk past me and not tell me what happened," she said, and I backpedaled over to where she was standing and got prepared to give her exactly what she wanted.

"Girl, you are not going to believe this shit." I leaned in closer to her and started running my mouth what seemed a thousand miles per minute.

She went from laughing, holding her stomach, to tears streaming down her face, and then her face bore a look of shock, but I was on such a roll, I didn't pay her any attention.

"I made her crazy ass write that letter and gave her

two good hotshots. Then, you know me. Since she dropped that damn cup—which I was mad about by the way—I had to clean up, so I went and grabbed the broom and swept up better than the—"

"I'ma beat ya fuckin' ass!" Tyleek's voice boomed from behind me, cutting off my sentence, and I swear all the color drained from my face. It was then I looked up and noticed Desiree's face, which quickly changed after she saw my face. She was trying her hardest not to laugh at me, but I guess she couldn't hold it in. Ugh, she made me sick.

"I told you he was gon' spank dat ass!" she screamed before she burst out laughing—her and Trapp, whose presence was made aware at the sound of his laughter.

"Get yo' ass up in that office!" Tyleek barked, and I spun around in the chair with puppy dog eyes, but then locked eyes once again with Tyquan. Ah damn.

Firm

Ki'Asia was hardheaded as hell. I stood there for a good minute and listened to her go on about how she killed Tricie. I felt no sympathy for Tricie whatsoever, don't get me wrong, but Ki'Asia just would not fuckin' listen. I already knew Tricie's ass wasn't pregnant because the damn female she had pretending to be pregnant was none other than Denice.

When I met Denice, I saw that her ass was, once again, pregnant, and she informed me how that came about. She stated that she had found out she was a little over a month and was going to terminate the pregnancy until Tricie offered her half a million dollars to keep the baby and pass it off as hers. Denice had just moved back to town, and considering she didn't have a doctor here, it was easy for her to use Tricie's information at a new doctor that neither of them were familiar with, get an ID, and assume Tricie's identity.

As time went on, Tricie slipped up and said my name around Denice, and once she confirmed it was indeed the same person, that was when she reached out to me. So now the dilemma was since I told her to continue to go along with the plan, I felt bad that she was going to be out of the half a mil she was promised since a dead woman couldn't pay, and I had to cough that shit up outta my pocket. I swear Ki'Asia's ass was just damn hardheaded.

"Get yo' ass up in this office!" I screamed on Ki'Asia. She turned around to me, and I could see the puppy dog eyes she used when she wanted to get her way, but the shit wasn't working this time. Before she could get up from the barstool, her face went blank.

"Damn, ma. That's what it is now. You can't speak?" some nigga said from behind me. I really wasn't in the mood for this shit today.

I heard Trapp sigh before Desiree said, "Oh shit!"

"Tyquan, what you want? What can I do for you?" Ki'Asia asked as she leaned back against the bar, and I looked at her like she really had bumped her fucking head.

"So you didn't just hear me tell you to take ya *fuckin' ass upstairs to that office!*" I yelled, causing Desiree to flinch and tears to form in Ki'Asia's eyes.

"My man, you ain't gotta talk to her like that!" the nigga had the audacity to bark behind my back. Ki'Asia and Desiree were the only ones that could see the smirk that appeared on my face, and whereas Desiree's eyes widened, Ki'Asia shook her head, and I heard a hammer being cocked, and I knew it was Trapp.

Slowly, I turned around, and the smirk I was wearing had turned into a full-fledged smile... right before I laid his ass out.

"Now get yo' ass upstairs," I turned to Ki'Asia and said. "And Trapp, take out the trash. I don't give a fuck who he is or why he decided to involve himself in my damn business. Take the trash out!"

Half the day was already gone, and the rest of the day wasn't going to get any better. As we walked toward—well as I walked and Ki'Asia waddled toward the elevator, I thought about how I was going to bring up the conversation of Denice to her without her feeling like I was keeping secrets. Not only that, but I had set it up for Denice to run by the club today to meet with us because I knew for a fact me telling Ki'Asia this off-the-wall shit was not going to be believable if she didn't hear it from the horse's mouth.

The elevator ride up to the third floor was quiet, and I knew she knew I was mad as hell. I told her little ass to stand down and let me handle shit, but she just had to get her hands dirty someway, somehow. The thing that scared me about her was she was really batshit crazy, and I didn't know what the hell made her that way. I made a mental note to ask her aunt since I didn't really deal with her moms like that. Maureen was off and on. One minute she fucked with you, and the next minute it was fuck you. I didn't have time for her flip-flopping ass, so I'd just ask Chan and see if I could get it out of her.

When we reached the office, Ki'Asia sat down behind her desk, and I took a seat at the chair in front of it, staring at her intently before running my hand down my face.

"Ma... I told you I had it. What the hell is wrong with you?" I asked her.

"You told me you had it. You told me she wasn't pregnant by you. You told me you wasn't worried about the baby. But you wasn't telling me shit, Firm! All that talking and you wasn't saying shit. So... I handled it. No biggie!" she said all nonchalantly like it really wasn't no big deal. When I gave her ass this half a mil debt that I was now in that I should make her ass pay, I wanted to see if it was still no big deal.

"Well, Ms. I Gotta Have My Hands Involved In Everything, let's see how you like it—" My phone vibrating cut off my conversation. Trapp let me know that someone named Denice was here to see me, but evidently, Ki'Asia had already peeped it on the camera, because she had a scowl on her face. I shot him a text and told him to escort her up.

"Perfect. I got someone—"

"Who the fuck is Trapp getting on the elevators with, Firm?"

"That's what I wan—"

"So you really think I'm wrapped tight, huh? I just gotta keep making examples outta people, huh?" She sat there, mumbling shit under her breath, and I just shook my head. I was really starting to think something was wrong with this girl aside from just your typical hood crazy. Nah, there was really an underlying issue with her.

Trapp tapped on the door before walking in with Denice. Now, I didn't mention it, but Denice was bad as fuck. Any nigga with eyes could see that. Even with her being pregnant, that did little to nothing to keep from bricking a nigga's dick up when she walked by... except for mine. Dammit, I knew better.

She stood at about five six, was brown skinned, kept her hair in a short cut with red and blonde highlights, had a mole above her full, lickable lips, thick eyebrows with a perfect arch, and eyelashes that damn near touched them shits. And her body? My God! Tricie was a thick little something, but she ain't had shit on Denice. With all that going on in the looks department, shorty was the biggest whore walking the earth. She was now four kids, four baby daddies in, and it had been four years since I'd seen her. Damn children were in stepladders.

"Come in and cl—"

"You don't run this shit, Tyleek! I. Did. Not. Tell. That. Bitch. To. Step. Foot. In. My. Muthafuckin'. Office. Did I!" Ki'Asia said. She had stood up and was headed in Denice's direction, and both my eyes and Trapp's had widened because this was the third time I had seen her eyes turn coal black. Whatever the fuck was going on with baby girl was scaring the shit out of me. Nobody was going to tell me this shit was normal.

I jumped up and grabbed her before she could reach Denice, but the smirk on Denice's face gave Ki'Asia strength that not even I was prepared for, and before I could get ahold of the situation, Ki'Asia had slipped from my grip and Denice's head was hitting the wall. That was it.

When Denice's head bounced forward from the wall, it bounced into Ki'Asia's fists... repeatedly. Denice, not being a soft chick by any means and having weight and height on Ki'Asia, she *attempted* to go head up, but that didn't work out too well. Lil' mama was like a raging lion until my shock wore off, and I was finally able to gently grab her without causing her harm. And when I did, I was more determined than ever to reach out to Chan or take her ass to mental health my damn self because her eyes were back hazel and she was smiling hard as hell.

"Ki'Asia... please go sit down and let me explain who

this is... please," I said, out of breath and pleading with my eyes.

She waddled back behind the desk, rubbing her stomach.

"Trapp, can you tell Desiree to send me up some hot wings and a salad and a tea? I'm hungry." Trapp looked at me and his face wore the same look of shock that mine had a moment ago. I just nodded toward the door for him to go ahead and go and signaled for Denice to have a seat. I didn't give a fuck that her face was turning colors or none of that. I wanted this shit to be over with.

"So how can I help you?" Ki'Asia asked with her hands folded in front of her with her undivided attention on Denice. Denice looked at me with a 'is this bitch crazy?' look.

"Ki, let me explain a little bit to you and fill in the blanks of what you don't already know." For the next half an hour, I explained Denice's part in everything, and although Ki'Asia didn't completely soften up, I could tell she felt a little like an ass for jumping the gun so quickly on both ends.

"OK. First, let me apologize, Denice. It is completely out of my character for me to just attack someone," Ki'Asia said just as Trapp was bringing her food in the office, and he had to chuckle. She shot him a look with a smirk that made him back down and head back out.

"But I do have a question. Like... what is your connection with Firm? It's obvious y'all know each other since you were able to reach out to him." Now that was the part I didn't tell her.

"Tyleek and I dated some years ago. I won't sit here and sugarcoat shit. I am what I am, and I'm a straight up whore, no chaser. Firm was too good for me. He caught me in an 'uncompromising' situation and left my ass alone. What he didn't know was that the best friend I always told him about but he had never met was none other than Tricie.

Tricie played that good girl role, but she was just as scandalous as I was. Difference between me and her, she couldn't have kids, and my ass stayed getting knocked up. She was nowhere near gullible, and you can best believe that. And the bitch's parents had more money than mine," she said, rolling her eyes. I knew Denice was mad about the situation with Ki'Asia and wanted to pop off, but she also knew who Ki'Asia was and who I was, so she knew that was an automatic death wish.

"Well, Ms. Denice, I thank you for coming in and explaining, but you can leave now. Run along," Ki'Asia stated, shooing her away as she began digging in her hot wings.

"I will when I'm finished. I really came here to see Firm, not explain this situation to you. He could have clearly did that his damn self, but..." Seeing Ki'Asia stand up and step out of her shoes and come from around the desk trailed her conversation off.

"What else you got to say, huh? 'Cause it's obvious you want these hands for real, and I'm inclined to give you what you want. Now the next time, trust and believe, Firm and nobody else will be able to keep me off you. They'll be taking yo' ass outta here on a gurney. Is that what you want, Denice? I can make it happen," Ki'Asia said with her hands on her hips and her head tilted to the side. I really think this girl forgot she was carrying my damn seed.

"Ki'Asia, go sit yo' ass down, and I ain't gon' say it

again!" I barked. I didn't wanna come off like that on her in front of ole girl, but she was pissing me the fuck off, and I was tired of her acting like she ain't had no damn sense. Well... I ain't know if it was an act or not, but still.

She looked me up and down like she was ready to try me, and honestly, I knew she probably was.

She burst out laughing and started clapping her hands and shaking her head. "Firm, you might be the nigga out in the streets, but this shit here is mine. You and her both can get the fuck out, nigga! Better yet, do that!" Ki'Asia said, still laughing as she went and sat back behind the desk, and I sat back down in the seat and ignored her ass.

"Go ahead and say what you needed to say, Denice, and make the shit quick. Don't get cute, 'cause I won't let her touch you again since she's carrying my child, and my child's wellbeing is first, but I'll put yo' ass to sleep with no questions asked."

Denice looked over at me with her mouth dropped as if she was shocked I had just spoken to her like that.

"Well, I overheard some dudes in High Point, my daughter's father and his crew in particular, saying they were going to make a move on you. In addition, the name 'Murda' is starting to be affiliated with you as well, from what I heard my father say." That caught Ki'Asia's attention.

"Who's your father?"

"The D.A.," Denice looked at her and said.

"Timothy Barnwright is your father?" Ki'Asia asked as she squinted her eyes at Denice. "Ohhhhh shit! Denice, Denice, Denice! Sister name Denisha, momma named Darlene. The three D's! Aw, damn! How didn't I see it before?" Ki'Asia laughed, hitting her desk. "You don't remember me? I've been at all the galas and events. I'm *that* Ki'Asia that works for Jackson Brown. I'm the top paralegal for the past four years," Ki'Asia cheerfully said like she hadn't just beaten the hell out of this girl damn near an hour ago.

"Oh my God! It damn sure is! This a small ass world," Denice said, and just that fast, the two of them forgot they were just trying to kill each other. Well, Denice's was more on the end of because she didn't want to get her ass whipped again, but Ki'Asia's crazy ass really had let it go.

She just didn't give a damn.

"OK, enough of this shit. Denice, what does your father know about Murda?" I questioned.

Denice told Ki'Asia what she'd overheard her father saying, and both of us were surprised that it had skipped over Jackson's head, and I was surprised Black hadn't mentioned anything about it. Denice said a little bit more before I dismissed her.

Now that we were alone again, Ki'Asia sat there with the puppy dog eyes.

"Before you start going in, Tyleek, I'm—"

I threw my hand up. She'd been cutting me off all day, and now it was my turn. When I looked up at her, she had tears running down her face. This girl was gon' be the damn death of me.

"What you crying for, ma?"

"Because you're mad at me, and I'm trying to apologize. I'm sorry. I got a little carried away. I didn't mean any harm, I really didn't," she said, and I knew she hadn't, but she really needed to learn to back down and let me lead. She was having a hard ass time doing that.

"Aight, ma. You ain't gotta cry."

Her face beamed, and she jumped up from behind her desk and wobbled over to me then sat in my lap. "I got some good news for you. I know where all them niggas lay their heads at. Each and every one of 'em. I know their names, their mama's names, sisters' names—hell, even the dogs' names." I just looked at her.

"What you talkin' about, Ki?"

"Dreek's team. I've been doing my own inve—"

"Didn't I tell ya fuckin' ass to stand down!" I yelled, causing her to flinch and burst out in tears. *God, please let this girl have this baby. I can't deal with this emotional ass Ki'Asia too much longer. I swear I can't.*

"OK, baby, I'm sorry. I didn't mean to yell. Thank you for getting me the information. But please, ma, I don't want you in the middle of this. OK?" I lifted her chin with my finger, and she nodded her head up and down.

"Okaaaaay. I was just trying to help." She got up off my lap, and I slapped her ass lightly as she headed back to her seat and slid me a folder before doggin' her wings, salad, and tea without asking did I want any. I mean, she straight smashed all of it in my face and didn't even take a breather to say 'want a bite?'

After she finished eating and went to the bathroom, she came back out and asked, "So what's the game plan?"

I looked at her, and she threw her hands up in surrender before she burst out laughing.

Chapter 10

"No one ever won a game by resigning."

Ki'Asia

It was my motherfucking birthday and my baby shower, and who was excited as hell was me! Dreek's entire team was gone, gone, gone, and everything was back to normal. The only thing wrong in my world was my aunt Chan's health. What she didn't tell me when I was in New York was that she had been diagnosed with end-stage kidney disease, and there was nothing else the doctors could do for her.

When she first told me, I ended up in the hospital due to a spike in my blood pressure, which they thought was causing the baby fetal distress. Tyleek told me if I killed his child, he would kill me and bring me back to life to impregnate me and kill me again. I was just so hurt. It was no secret that Chan and I were closer than my mother and I were, and I just couldn't bear the news of her not being here with me any longer.

Since my mother found out I was pregnant, she had been coming around a lot more, but she was still bipolar as ever, with her on and off ass. For the most part though, anything dealing with Ty'Asia brought her joy. Yes, we decided to name our little mama Ty'Asia Yanese, a combination of my, Tyleek's, and Taysia's name, and even a mixture of my and Anise's name since her first name was so similar to my middle name.

"You ready, big mama?" Tyleek came in the room and asked as I sat at the vanity applying my lip gloss. I was dressed in a pink long-sleeved romper that Anise had custom made for me, with some low comfortable wedges. My hair was good and thick and had grown at least three more inches, so the only thing I could do with it was pull a headband around it and let it flow down my back.

"I am, baby daddy." He grabbed me by my hand to help me stand and placed a 'Beautiful Mom' sash around me before gently kissing my lips.

"Aye, don't mess up my gloss, boy," I told him, playfully nudging his arm.

This baby had changed me in the last few months, and

for the good. Between knowing I was getting ready to be someone's mother and the death sentence my aunt was issued, I was looking at life a little differently. I wouldn't say I had done a 180, but I had at least done a 90 for the sake of my little one. The only illegal thing I had my hands in was taking the trips to meet the connect.

Tyleek and I drove to The Ballantyne Hotel where the baby shower was being held. Trust and believe, that was my bourgeois ass mama's idea. Hell, I could have had it at the club, which my birthday party was for sure being held there after the shower.

When we got there, I was amazed at the turnout. I mean, everyone I'd met over the years from the mayor and his wife, the district attorney, judges, radio personalities, everyone was in attendance, and of course it caused me to get emotional. Even Denice's ass was here, and she had already had the baby and half a mil richer. Her info ended up not doing shit to help us, but aye, that was neither here nor there in a good and bad way. The gift tables were overflowing with gifts for Ty'Asia, and both Tyleek and I were completely overwhelmed with joy and gratitude.

I sat in the center of the room as we played different games and ate little finger sandwiches and other hors d oeuvres that my mother had served. *Lord, can I please get some fried chicken with some baked macaroni and cheese, potato salad, rice with gravy, cornbread, collard greens, cabbage, candied yams, or even some ox tail, peas and rice, plantain, and callaloo, please, Lord, please! Anything but these damn pigs in a blanket and sandwiches no bigger than my fingernails!*

Tyleek must have noticed the frustration and discomfort on my face, because he rubbed my back but had the nerve to chuckle. I'd tread thin if I was him.

We sat there for the next two hours opening gift after gift, and I was exhausted and hadn't even moved. Ty'Asia had everything she needed for the next five years of her life—even money!

"Alright. Baby girl, we have a surprise for you. Tyleek, please turn her chair toward the entrance," my mother said on the mic as she stood at the back of the room.

I looked up at Tyleek, and he did as my mother requested, and I looked over at Desiree, Trapp, and

Da'Jon, and all of them wore silly smiles on their faces. Everyone I loved that could be here was here, so unless they were rolling my dream car through that door, I didn't see what more of a surprise I could be getting. When the doors opened, I had to squint my eyes to make sure they weren't deceiving me before the waterworks started. There standing before me were my aunt Chan, my cousin Mack, and Asaada. I broke out in the ugly cry.

"Oh my God, oh my God, oh my God! Noooo, I cannot believe this." I started crying harder and fanning myself, but I was too stuck to move. They started slowly walking toward me, and I truly thought I was in a dream.

"Surprise, princess," my aunty said when she made it over to me as she leaned over and kissed my forehead. She had lost so much weight since the last time I'd seen her, but she was still as beautiful as ever.

I stood and held her as tight as my stomach would allow, crying as I rocked back and forth, holding onto her. When I released her from my embrace, we both had tears in our eyes, and as I looked around, there was barely a dry eye in the room.

Tyleek, who I hadn't even noticed was no longer by my side, appeared with a microphone and gave it to my aunt.

"For those who are not aware of who I am, my name is Chan Barron, and I am Ki'Asia's aunt. This princess has been like a daughter to me from the time she was born. She may have come from her mother's womb, but she was definitely my daughter." She looked over at my mother, and I saw the glance the two of them exchanged. Well, couldn't argue with facts.

"Ki'Asia Synese Barron, you have always been special. You were a princess before you were born, a princess from the time you took your first step, and everything you've done in life thus far, you've done it royally. No one can hold a match to you, baby girl. And now you're becoming a queen, and Ty'Asia will become the princess.

I'm not even worried about the type of mother you will be because you protect those you love with everything in you, so I know your child will be your number one priority. Love her, cherish her, do right by her, and teach her better than what you were taught, baby girl." She removed the mic from her hand and whispered in my ear, "This game don't love nobody. Get out, now, Ki'Asia."

For some reason, her voice sent chills down my spine, but her smile contradicted her words. I brushed it off and gave her a smile that matched hers along with a hug, and everyone started clapping.

***

"And we don't buy no drinks at the bar, we pop champagne 'cause we got that dough, let me hear you say ah (ahh, ahh, ahh, ahh), you want me say ahh (ahh, ahh, ahh, ahh)!"

Trey Songz sung as we all danced up in VIP. Well, they danced, and I wobbled from side to side, waving my hands in the air. Even my aunt came out with us, and we were having a damn ball! My twenty-third birthday was going down as one of the best in history.

After Trey's performance, the lighting in the club went dim, and a projector screen released from the ceiling in the middle of the VIP section, but it was also showing on the TV's throughout the club. On the screen were images from my mother in the delivery room with my aunt and father there beside her, and many of my milestones throughout the years, up until the opening of *Touch of Class Nightclub*. I didn't know I had any more tears to release, but they were steadily streaming down my face. This was the best birthday ever.

After the film went off, the club went crazy, and Jeezy came out performing "Put On." From there, it was a wrap. And it was a wrap for me as well. By two o'clock, I was spent, and everyone around me was drunk as hell.

By the grace of God and all his protectors, we made it home, but I didn't sleep peacefully at all that night. I was in pain and tossed and turned until the pain became unbearable.

At nine o'clock, I woke Tyleek up.

"Babe, I can't take it no more. I'm in pain."

"What kind of pain, ma? What you talking 'bout?" He jumped straight up like the bed was on fire.

"I'm having contractions, babe."

"It's too early. You only eight months." I gave him a look and he jumped out the bed and called the doctor.

"How far apart are the contractions, ma?"

"They're about four minutes now," I told him as another one hit, bringing them down to three minutes. Once he relayed that to the doctor, a few seconds later, he was throwing the phone, giving me a quick sponge bath, washing himself off, grabbing my bag and the baby bag, and we were headed out the door to Carolina's Medical Center.

On the way to the hospital, I was texting everybody, letting them know I thought it was time. The only person that hadn't responded was my aunt, and that kind of had me worried.

"Tyleek, where did my aunt go last night?" I asked him.

"She had a room at Ballantyne, babe. Wassup?" he glanced over at me and asked.

"Nothing. I texted her to tell her we were on our way to the hospital, and she didn't text back. Mack ain't text back yet either."

"Don't worry about it, babe. Ya aunt let loose last night, her and Mack, so they probably both still sleep," he said, and kissed my hand to reassure me.

"Yeah, you're right. Oh my *Godddddddd! Hurry up!*" I screamed as it felt like my insides were being ripped apart.

By the time we made it to the hospital and they got me on the stretcher, they were taking me straight to Labor and Delivery. The nurse thought I didn't hear her non-whispering ass say that I was nine and half centimeters dilated and couldn't get an epidural, but I heard her loud and clear. I wanted to kill her!

My mother didn't make it to the hospital in time, but Tyleek and Desiree were right by my side when I pushed out my 7-pound, 9-ounce princess, who came in the world screaming her head off. I mean she was hollering for dear life. As soon as they laid her on my chest, she stopped screaming. Nothing could have prepared me for this moment. She was an exact replica of Tyleek until she opened her eyes. And once she did that, she was all me.

"My baby," I cried, and for the first time ever, I saw Tyleek release tears of joy.

Once they got her cleaned up and placed her in his arms, I knew right then she was going to be as much of a daddy's girl as I was.

While Tyleek was in the middle of his bonding session, his phone went off and he asked Desiree to get it for him. She whispered something in his ear and then smiled at me before he handed me Ty'Asia, hopped up out the chair, and flew out the room.

"Desiree, what the fuck is going on?"

Firm

Nothing could prepare a man for seeing his child being brought into the world. If I never had respect for women before, I respected them to the utmost now, especially my queen. She handled that shit like a champ. There was no cursing me out, belittling me, or any of that. She leaned on me and allowed me to comfort her throughout the entire process of bringing baby girl into the world. She was for damn sure a trooper.

When I looked in Ty'Asia's eyes, I fell in love for the second time in my life. I knew right then and there these two women would have me wrapped around their fingers, and I'd kill for them at the drop of a dime. She was my little mini-me with her mother's hazel eyes, and I even prayed she had her mother's feisty personality. As batshit crazy as Ki'Asia was, she loved and loved hard and protected those she loved with everything in her.

My phone vibrating broke my concentration, and I started not to answer it, but I forgot I hadn't reached out to my father, Taysia, or Anise, and thought it could be one of them. I told Desiree to grab it since I had little mama in my arms. It was a good thing I was alert and had a grip on my baby because what she whispered in my ear almost knocked the wind out of me. I handed Ty'Asia to Ki and ran up out the room.

As soon as I got in the hallway, Mack was pacing up and down the hall. When he looked at me, tears were welled up in his eyes.

"Come on, son."

I followed behind him and we jumped on the elevator. He didn't utter a word to me, and I was too speechless to talk. When we got to the room Chan was in, I was scared to go in, afraid of what I would see, but Mack said she needed to speak with me and it was urgent and she didn't have much time left, so that put fire under my ass.

Once I opened and closed the door, I walked to toward her bed, and from just some hours, she'd looked like a shell of the woman she was previously.

"Sit, Firm. Ahem. I need to tell you something."

I sat in the chair closest to her bed and pulled it directly beside her since it was evident she couldn't talk loud. This shit was killing me. How the fuck was I gon' tell Ki'Asia this shit, man?

"Have you seen Ki'Asia go dark?" she asked, and I nodded my head, remembering I wanted to speak with her about it some months back.

"Take her to get the help she needs that she never got. When Ki'Asia was five, she was raped by her grandfather. We don't know how long it had been going on because she shut down for a while after that and clung solely to her father. I mean, she clung to him for dear life. And it was strange because Ki'Asia loved her grandfather just as much as she loved Divine.

One summer, she and Da'Jon went upstate to visit their grandparents, and Divine kept saying he had a funny feeling this particular day..." She coughed and pointed to the water beside her bed. I fixed her a cup of water and she took slow sips before she resumed.

"He said he had a funny feeling this particular day. Made us hop in the car with him to travel seven hours upstate to Buffalo for a funny feeling. We were glad he did.

When we got to their house, Ki'Asia was holding her

grandfather's sac in her hand and had stuffed his penis in his mouth. We wouldn't have been able to find out what happened, but Ki'Asia being the outspoken child she always was didn't hold back on what she'd done. She said she did to him what he *made* her do to him, which was play with his balls and suck his shriveled-up dick—her words.

Maureen was upset with Ki'Asia for years. She was as much of a daddy's girl as Ki'Asia was, but she eventually got over it, understanding that her child came first. But she hated Divine because he killed her mother in front of her face for allowing it to happen. Honestly, I think that's why..."

Chan began coughing uncontrollably, and the machines she were hooked up to began to beep loudly. Mack rushed into the room, and a team of nurses and doctors barged in shortly after, yelling for us to get out.

Mack was inconsolable, and truthfully, I was at a loss for words after what Chan had just told me. She didn't even need to finish the statement for me to know that's the reason they had left New York. I put two and two together, remembering Divine saying he moved to Charlotte because he wanted to expand and for other reasons.

I headed back to the room in a daze. October 29, 2010, one day after my girl's twenty-third birthday, we gave birth to our daughter, and she lost her aunt who was more like her mother, and I found out something she'd been holding inside for years.

By the time I got back to the room, Maureen, Walt, Asaada, Desiree, Trapp, Pop, and Raquan were there. I looked in Raquan's eyes and dropped my head. He was confused, but I motioned my head for him to follow me out into the hallway. When he got out there and I explained to him what had just happened, he broke down. Pop must have heard him because he came flying out the room, and when he saw the tears in my eyes, he mouthed 'Chan,' and all I could do was nod my head. We stood there in silence until Raquan was able to gather himself for us to go back in there and break the news to Ki'Asia. One of the happiest days of our lives ended up being one of the worst days of hers.

***

Ki'Asia hated to leave Ty'Asia with my sisters while

we came to New York, but she refused to not say bye to Chan. Mack opted to have his mother cremated. He said he wanted her with him at all times instead of having to go visit her at a burial site, and I definitely understood him.

I hadn't mentioned anything to Ki'Asia about what Chan told me, but I felt now was the best time. I saw her slipping further away from reality, and I couldn't allow that to happen.

After the memorial service, we went back to Chan's house and went up to the room we stayed in when we came to visit the first time. We both kicked our shoes off and laid back on the bed to get comfortable.

"Ma, I need to talk to you about something," I said to her as she laid her head on my chest.

"I'm listening."

"I know about what happened with your grandfather," I said, and I could feel her heart rate increasing rapidly.

"Who told you?" she asked in a shaky voice.

"Chan told me before she passed away. I know shit between us moved fast so you probably feel like that's why you could never tell me, but I want you to know I don't feel no type of way about that shit. I'm still gon' be here for you. It doesn't make me love you any less, and I don't look at you any differently, you hear me?"

I looked down at her, and she was looking up at me with tears in her eyes.

"I wanna get better, Tyleek, I do. I loved my grandfather, but I also knew what he did to me wasn't right. I was young, but I was far from anyone's dummy. I've never been a stupid girl. I felt like his reason for loving me was to molest me, if that makes sense. And believe it or not, I thought when I got older, I wouldn't want to experience sexual relations with a man because of what he did, but I didn't allow it to control me.

What I did to *him* is what controlled me. I enjoyed it too much. The kill. The excitement I felt behind it. It scared me and fascinated me at the same time. And to this day, I can't explain *why* I enjoy torturing and killing as much as I do, but I don't think I'll ever stop."

I didn't know how to respond to that. I'd seen Ki'Asia in action. I'd seen the excitement that she was speaking so passionately about. Yet, I didn't see her any differently.

"I ain't no psychiatrist or no shit like that, ma, so I can't give you no professional advice, but at that moment, I don't see no wrong in what you did. You defended yourself. Do you know how many children are victimized and not able to defend themselves, and that sexual abuse goes on for years and ends up fucking with that child's mental and sometimes repeats itself? You did what you had to do. Now... the ongoing scares the shit out of me, but you can get through this, ma. Together, me and you will get through this, you hear me?"

She looked at me with tears in her eyes. "I believe you, Tyleek, and I know we will. Thank you for everything, babe... for believing in me, being there for me, not turning your back on me, giving me your heart, and most importantly, giving me the one precious thing that could turn my world around. For Ty'Asia, I'm gonna be better," she said before kissing me briefly and laying her head back on my chest.

We laid in silence for a while before her light snores

could be heard.

"I love you, Ki'Asia Barron-Ditmas," I whispered, then kissed her forehead gently before letting sleep catch me as well.

Chapter 11

"The most powerful weapon in chess is to have the next move."

Firm

It had been three and a half years since all the drama with Dreek's team, the birth of our baby girl, the death of Ki'Asia's aunt Chan, and things had been going great. I couldn't complain at all. After I found out what happened with Ki'Asia in her youth and explained to her I wasn't going anywhere, our bond had strengthened even more. She continued to do her thing with the clubs and funeral home but let the butcher shop go. She had enough on her plate with them girls at the strip club, and she still was making runs out of country to her pop's connect, which reminded me, she was in for more than a few surprises when she came home from Peru.

This morning, Trapp, Desiree, and I went to Ballantyne Jeweler's, and I copped her a 5-carat cushion cut diamond engagement ring, of course with the help of Desiree. Her ass wouldn't let me pick the ring out on my own, like I didn't know my girl's taste. Her birthday was still six months away, and I was going to propose to her then, but I decided to do something big this weekend at the club and let it be a surprise engagement party. Again, Desiree wanted to take over that as well, and I let her rock out.

As bad as I wanted to make Ki'Asia my wife, I knew that she would never marry me without Divine being present. What she didn't know since she was in Peru was that her father was on his way home, so this was the perfect time for me to pop the question to her. I'd already gotten his approval and assured him I would do it with him there. This engagement ring or a wedding meant nothing to me anyway aside from a title. In every way that mattered, Ki'Asia Barron-Ditmas was already my wife.

When we left the jewelry store, I hit up Maureen and told her what was going on, and she seemed to be excited. Since Ki'Asia had given birth to Ty, her and Maureen's relationship had gotten somewhat better. It still was nowhere near the perfect mother/daughter relationship, but

I could honestly say Maureen was one hell of a grandmother toward Ty'Asia. I then called up Taysia and Anise and told them about it, and they were thrilled as well. Anise said she wanted to plan it, and I gave her Desiree's phone number. I wasn't getting in the middle of that shit. I'd let them two argue it out.

"Man, you ready for this?" Trapp asked as we pulled up to my old crib which was his crib now and walked into the living room.

"Nigga, I was born ready. That's my world right there. I mean, she mean as hell, feisty, and batshit crazy, but I can't see life without her, you feel me?"

"I got you, man. Sis cool as fuck anyway. Always have been. Sheeiittt, maybe I'll settle down one day. Her homegirl cool too, she just loud and mean, and I swear she like to fight and fuck at the same time, bruh," he said, and I couldn't help but laugh. Over the last four years, Desiree had become like another sister to me, and her mouth was unfiltered, her hands were a weapon, and she rode with my girl the long way. If you didn't see me with Ki'Asia, you didn't see her without Desiree. You could best believe that.

"She definitely cool, man. I don't know about marriage, 'cause she might fuck you up, fam!"

"Yeah, gone 'head wit' that. Anyway, you ever think about leaving this shit alone, bruh? I mean, you got the construction company, your girl got three damn clubs and a funeral home... Y'all sitting on money out the ass. What's the purpose of continuing to risk your life for this shit, bruh? You know these streets don't love nobody, and we lost a lot over the years.

Honestly, after I killed that nigga Branden, I was ready to leave this shit then, but I'd be damned if I left you hanging. You've been my nigga, and I'ma ride it out wit' you 'til the wheels fall off. But do you ever get tired of it?" Trapp asked.

Truthfully speaking, I did, especially since I took over as the role of Murda. I mean, don't get me wrong, my shit was solidified before I even joined with Ki'Asia, but she was running shit on a whole other level. I didn't see how she was doing it along with everything else she had going on in her life. And it wasn't an average empire. Every damn thing was accounted for from the drugs to the murders to the greasing of palms. All her I's were dotted and her T's were crossed. She didn't miss a beat with that shit.

"I do, man, I ain't gon' front. But how I tell my girl that I want her to back down completely from the one thing that she refuses to give up? This shit ain't just about the hustle for her, Trapp. This shit is her life. Where some little girls grow up wanting to be a princess, a ballerina, ya know, the girly shit, Ki'Asia always wanted to be a hustler. How the fuck I take that away from her? How I tell her what our net worth is and let her see we never have to push another drug on the streets of any city, and our grandchildren's children will still be eating? Man, she ain't trying to hear that," I told Trapp.

I wasn't dealing with the average female. Ki'Asia was truly one person who was made for this. The money and moves could be made in her sleep. As successful as she was in everything else in life, backing down from this just wasn't going to be an easy thing for her to do. Even though she was only making trips in and out of country, holding on to just that one little thing kept her in the game.

“Firm, you gotta get her to understand, man. This game is temporary. It ain’t no permanent success in this shit. You get what you can and you get the fuck out. She had a successful run. You had a successful run. Together, y’all had a damn successful run. And y’all are still successful without it. The outcome is death or jail—you know this.”

I thought about was Trapp said, and he was absolutely right. But regardless of what, it was easier said than done for her. I was getting ready to respond when I heard my phone go off. Pulling it out, I saw it was Ms. Berniece. Ms. Berniece had been lil’ mama’s babysitter since she was three months old and was now basically part of the family.

“Hey, Ms. Berniece. What’s up?”

“Hi, Mr. Ditmas. I’m sorry to bother you. Little Ms. Ty’Asia has a slight fever and she’s real fussy. I think she may have a stomach virus because she’s pooping all over the place too. I don’t have any Pedialyte here. Can you run by the drug store and bring some over, if you don’t mind?”

I didn’t want little mama fussing and getting on Ms. Berniece nerves, and I ain’t had shit else to do for the day, so I just decided to cut my time short with Trapp and head over to get her.

"I'll be through there to get her, Ms. Berniece."

"Oh, no. I don't want to inconvenience you. You can just bring it by," she said.

"Nah, I wanna spend some time with my little munchkin anyway. I don't like daddy's little princess being sick and fussy," I told her as I dapped Trapp up and mouthed I'd get at him later before I headed out the door.

"OK, if you insist. But you know it's no problem."

"I know. I'll be there shortly." I disconnected the call and headed over to CVS.

On my ride over, I thought about everything Trapp said and how I was ready to make this life change. Not just because of what he'd planted in my head, but I wanted to be the husband Ki'Asia needed and the father Ty'Asia deserved. I didn't want my daughter to ever have to grow up the way Ki'Asia grew up, with her father behind bars, and damn sure not six feet under. Ki'Asia shouldn't want that for her either, which I knew she didn't.

In the past three years, Ki'Asia took that mother role serious as hell. Nothing came before her little princess.

From mother/daughter dates, to shopping, to spending time reading books, tucking her in, Ki'Asia made sure that was all done by her. You would have thought Maureen was the perfect mother to Ki'Asia because that's what she was to Ty'Asia. She had even started going to counseling to work through her issues.

Surprisingly, Ki'Asia hadn't picked up a gun or torture tool since she killed Tricie, which said a lot for her. I tested her one night to see what she would do, and she said the thrill was gone. Go figure.

After I grabbed the medicine and Pedialyte and paid for it, I headed to Ms. Berniece's house to pick up little mama. When I got there, she was definitely running a fever and ran straight into my arms.

"Daddy, I want Mommy," she whined, laying her head on my chest.

Ki'Asia wasn't due back from Peru until tomorrow, which everyone knew, so she was going to have to tough it out with her pops tonight.

"Mommy will be back home tomorrow, baby girl. You gon' have to tough it out with Daddy tonight, princess," I told her, kissing her cheek. “OK, Ms. Bernice. Thanks a million. I’ll give you a call later if I need anything,” I told her and headed out the door with princess in my arms.

“OK, Mr. Ditmas. Feel better, my little Ty Ty,” Ms. Bernice said to Ty, calling her the nickname she’d given her.

“Bye bye, Ms. Banice.”

Once we got to the car, I strapped her in and we headed to the house. Ki’Asia was completely in love with the house I had built. She always joked that all she needed was a club and grocery store built on the property and she would never have to leave. I was looking into that for my queen.

By the time we got to the house, Ty was knocked out. I pulled in the driveway and ran inside to take the bags then came back out to the car to get her. As soon as I got her inside the house, I ran her a cool alcohol bath and gave her some Pedialyte.

It was obvious that my lovely queen had been home because she left her shoes in the middle of the bedroom floor, and I knew they weren’t there this morning before I left. *She must have come back a day early*, I thought to myself.

We stood at the bathroom sink, brushing our teeth and looking in the mirror, something we always did, when I thought I heard a noise downstairs. I didn't think anything of it since I knew Ki'Asia was back in town, but after a moment, she didn't come upstairs.

"I be right back, princess," I told Ty'Asia as I left out the bathroom and headed down the stairs.

When I reached the bottom of the steps and entered the living room, I was met with the shock of my life. I had been caught slipping in a big way by the last person I'd ever suspected.

"So this what we doing now? You in my fuckin' crib with a gun up to my fuckin' face, huh!" I barked, and anger consumed me. Without thinking, I charged, and the gun went off three times.

"Yo' stupid ass. Y'all thought this shit was over—"

"Daddy!" *Ty'Asia, baby, no!*

Pow, pow!

"Oh my God... Ty'Asia! What the fuck have I done!

She wasn't supposed to be here!" I heard the voice say, but I couldn't do anything. Everything was all fucked up.

Ki'Asia

I was glad to finally have landed back in Charlotte. One of the many things I hated about this game was having to fly out of the country to meet with the connect. But if I wanted the purest coke flooding through my clubs and in these streets, I couldn't get it from one of these niggas here. My father always instilled in me "it cost to be the boss," so sacrifices had to be made, and leaving Tyleek and Ty'Asia behind at times was one of them. I could have easily turned him on to my connect and let him make these trips, but I still had my hands too deep in this side of the game to turn it over completely.

Since I powered my phone off when I got on the plane, the first thing I did when I made it to my car was turn it back on. The phone wasn't on for two seconds, and I had what seemed to be a million and one text messages and voicemails. I skimmed through the texts to see which were important and noticed I had quite a few from Desiree. I quickly hit her back and told her I'd just landed but would be by the club as soon as I went home and showered. Firm wasn't expecting me back until tomorrow, and neither was Ms. Bernice, so I had a little bit of time to mess around at the club for a bit. Knowing Firm, he was out handling business and wasn't home anyway, so I could take a quick shower and be out the door.

When I made it home, just like I thought, Firm's car wasn't there. I grabbed the one bag I had, closed the garage, and headed into the house. Home sweet home, finally. It was good to know that Tyleek made sure he kept the house as clean while I wasn't here as if I were here. Nothing would have ruined my mood more than to come home to a dirty house. Noticing the mail on the counter, immediately, I spotted a letter from my pops and grabbed it before heading up the steps. Once I made it to my room, I kicked off my shoes and placed my duffel bag in the closet. I'd deal with unpacking later. After rummaging through my closet and grabbing my Levi jeans with the matching jacket and shirt and placing it on the bed, I went in the bathroom and turned the water on for my shower.

On the outside looking in, everyone thought I had this perfect life. Financially, things were great, but I so badly wanted to stop doing this, especially since I had Ty'Asia. I wanted to live like a normal person for once. Although I couldn't say 100 percent that my childhood was snatched from me, being the daughter of a hustler, the girl of a hustler, and then being pushed to run an empire, took its toll on me and forced me to grow up faster than my peers. I didn't want that life for my baby girl. True indeed, it didn't affect her now at all, but I knew in the long run, it definitely would.

As I showered, I thought of a way to tell my father that I no longer wanted to be doing this. I just wanted to run my clubs and open the after-hours childcare center for Ms. Bernice and two indoor trampoline parks for the kids. I also had some other things I wanted to do for the community. He and I never spoke of me stepping down completely, so I didn't know how he would take it.

After showering and throwing on my clothes, I was back out the door like I'd never came. As soon as I turned the engine on the Lexus, Chris Brown's "She Ain't You" came blasting through the speakers. Damn near forty minutes and one angry ass driver later, I was pulling up to

Touch of Class Nightclub. Before getting out the car, I grabbed good ole Rosie from the glove compartment and secured her in my waistband. I made sure to check my surroundings and lock the door when I got out the car. Over the years, I'd made a few enemies—well fans as I called them—and they loved to lurk around my clubs for some reason, which is why I made sure to stay strapped at all times.

When I walked in, I saw two of my top dancers engaged in a heated argument. Tessa, aka Chocolate Nasty, was my biggest money maker, and the last thing I needed was for her to be involved in any of the bullshit these other chicks had going on at the club. Serenity was a hell of a dancer, but she was expendable—trust and believe.

"Aye, aye, what's going on here?" I asked as I approached them. When Tessa turned in my direction, I could immediately tell that she had been crying. She was a beautiful thick chocolate girl and could work the pole like no other, but honestly, she didn't fit in this world. I didn't know her story and made it my business to never get close with any of the girls that worked here, because I knew my heart, but I did know without a shadow of a doubt that this life was not for her.

"Boss lady, she's been stealing from me all week. And Reese caught her red handed, but she won't 'fess up to it and give my money back," Tessa said before she started crying again.

"Aight, first off, Serenity, you know damn well I don't play that thieving shit. If you steal from one of your own, you'll damn sure steal from me, and we both know where that will leave you, right?"

She looked at me and rolled her eyes. See… this is what I didn't tolerate. I'd be damned if allowed a bitch that was beneath me to stand in my face and disrespect me. I'd never had to make an example out of one of these females, but Serenity was pushing it.

"You just automatically take her word for it without even trying to find out what's really going on. You didn't ask me did I take her money. You just jumping the gun, telling me what's gon' happen and all that like I can't go somewhere else to find a job."

Without thinking, I removed Rosie from my waistband

and put it directly under her chin.

"Who said anything about you going to find other employment, huh? You ever steal from me, and dancing will be an afterthought because ya ass won't be breathing. Now… you understood me that time? Do I have to revisit this shit again?" I questioned. I wished her ass would come out her face the wrong way.

"You got it, Ki," she said and walked off, but not before I snatched her ass by them tracks and pulled her back.

"I ain't finish. Don't walk off when adults are talking to you, little girl. Now what you are about to do is give this girl back her money. Guns don't faze you? Good. You gangsta, huh? But I promise you I'll beat yo' ass to death with my hands and walk out this muthafucka like ain't shit happen. Give that girl her damn money!" I screamed before letting her hair go, and she flinched. Who the hell wouldn't flinch when a gun was pressed to their chin, but flinched because someone raised their voice? I had to have one of the dumbest dancers on the east coast. Shorty must have had mommy issues.

She reached in her little backpack and handed Tessa what looked to be close to $8,000. My head snapped up, and my hand landed across her face so fast I scared my damn self. I couldn't believe she had stolen that much money from that girl.

"Have you lost your fucking mind!" I yelled. I saw Desiree coming down the steps of the club. She stood beside me, shaking her head with her arms folded across her chest.

"This the bullshit I had to deal with while you were gone. This ole thieving ass ho here," Desiree said, but I was still too stunned to even reply.

After gathering my thoughts, once the shock wore off, I dismissed Serenity real quick. It was no telling who all she had done that to. I apologized to Tessa and told her she needed to toughen up a little more and whip some ass, because if not, these girls were going to run all over her. I didn't know if she had any fight in her, but these jealous females up in here wasn't going to stop until they broke her, or she learned to stand up for herself.

Desiree and I headed up the steps to the office and went

over the books for the past week. Although Touch of Class really jumped on the weekends, considering it was one of the most elite gentlemen's clubs in Charlotte, business boomed throughout the week as well. The club was grossing every bit of $200k a week.

We sat there for the next hour and a half catching up on what had been going on over the past week in my absence. "So the only thing we need to do is—" Desiree went to say, but was cut off by the ringing of my phone.

I looked at the screen and saw it was Ms. Bernice calling. I was confused because, as far as she knew, I was still in Peru. But it was possible she saw me leaving the house considering she stayed four houses down from me.

"Hello, Ms. Bernice. How is my little sunshine doing?" I asked when I answered the phone.

"Oh my God, Ms. Barron. You have to come home. I'm so sorry to call you while you're away, but you have to get home now. Oh my God, Lord, please help them Father!" she yelled through her cries.

"Ms. Bernice, wait, whoa… What is going on? Is my baby OK?" I asked while running out of the office with

Desiree on my heels. I didn't know if she could hear Ms. Bernice or whether she saw the look on my face, but she didn't ask any questions as she followed out behind me.

Ms. Bernice continued to wail, and I could no longer understand what she was saying. Getting frustrated and having heard enough, I ended the call and jumped in my car as Desiree jumped in hers, and sped out of the parking lot. I turned the music off and prayed harder than I'd ever prayed before. I didn't know what was happening, but I'd never heard Ms. Bernice cry as hard as she was crying on the phone. I didn't know if something had happened to my baby girl or what. It dawned on me to call Tyleek, but I was shaking so bad, I couldn't focus on dialing his number and driving at the same time.

When I pulled up on my street, there were police cars everywhere, but particularly in front of my house. Without thinking, I left the car running and jumped out. I saw Tyleek's car in the driveway, and my heart damn near jumped out of my chest.

"Ma'am, I'm sorry, but you cannot go in there," an officer said to me, placing his hand on my shoulder.

"If you don't get your fucking hands off me, I promise you won't have them long," I responded to him through gritted teeth. Before he had a chance to say anything, Officer Black, one of the officers on my payroll, was telling him to let me in.

As soon as I stepped through the door, I froze. My body began shaking uncontrollably. Lying face down in front of me was the love of my life, my heartbeat, my soul, my everything. This could not be happening right now… it just couldn't be. I kneeled down beside him and, against the officers' and crime scene investigator's wishes, turned him over. I couldn't tell what happened to him, but there was blood pooling from everywhere.

"Firm, baby, get up. Do you hear me, Tyleek? Come on, baby. You can't leave me like this, man. Please don't leave me, please," I cried out. *God, why me?* This man was all I had. There was no life without him. He was my best friend, my lover, my confidant. He was my strength when I was weak. *Lord, I'm weak right now. I can't lose him*. I felt a hand on my back and heard sniffles and knew it was Desiree. All of a sudden, her soothing rubs to my back stopped.

"Jesus, no. Noooo, no, no, no, no!" I heard her yell.

I immediately stood up and looked at her, but she was looking off in another direction. From the corner of my eyes, I saw a man bent over on one knee. Through tears, I tried to focus on what it was he was looking at. When he stood up, a feeling ran through my body that couldn't be explained. What I was feeling was foreign to me. I knew I was about to lose it.

I slowly walked toward the direction where the guy had just stood up from, and with each step closer, my mind shifted and my heart broke. Desiree caught me before I could fall completely.

"God, nooooooooooooo! Ty'Asiaaaaa! Nooooo, not my baby, God, not my baby!" I shook uncontrollably as the last ounce of love I had left was removed from my body.

I needed to get out of here. The walls were closing in and I felt myself slipping into that place that I'd tried hard to pull myself from for the past couple years. Everything that I've worked so hard for no longer mattered. The person I tried so hard not to be was rearing her ugly head.

I just needed to accept the fact that me being destined for the greatness that others saw in me and wanted for me wasn't going to happen. I was who the fuck I was. I was *that* bitch. They wanted it? That was what they were about to get. *I pray the Queen City was ready to feel my wrath, because Ki'Asia Synese Barron will stop at nothing to avenge the death of my loved ones.*

With my last tear dropping and not a fuck to give, I walked out the door until I heard, "Get a gurney ASAP! Hurry up! We got a pulse over here!"

To be continued...

Connect with the author:

Author page:

https://www.facebook.com/sparkle.lewis.967

Like page:

https://www.facebook.com/AuthorSparkleLewis/

Website and blog:

https://authorsparklelewis.com/

Be sure to join my reading group, Sparkle's Reading Jewels:

https://www.facebook.com/groups/SparklesReadingJewels/

Be sure to LIKE our Major Key

Publishing page on Facebook!

CPSIA information can be obtained
at www.ICGtesting.com
Printed in the USA
LVHW05s0310010618
579226LV00008B/242/P